PRAISE

Sin Eaters uses an off-kilter approach to explore religion, faith, and the oddities of what it means to be human in a vast world beyond our grasp. These rich, highly imagined stories are deeply felt and emotionally resonant with a humor that sneaks up on you.

> —JULIE IROMUANYA, assistant professor of English (creative writing and Africana literature) and director of undergraduate studies for the Program in Creative Writing at the University of Chicago. 2021 Permafrost Prize judge.

Who is Caleb Tankersley and what business does he have writing a debut story collection this excellent? *Sin Eaters* is haunted by the ghost of Flannery O'Conner, as well as contemporary power-houses like Kelly Link and George Saunders, all the while giving us something wholly original, something I can only describe as 'Tankersleyian.' By turns magical and mundane, hilarious and heartbreaking, these stories herald the arrival of a wonderful new writer whose books I will greet with excitement and anticipation for years to come. Stop reading this blurb and start reading these stories immediately.

> —ANDREW MALAN MILWARD, author of *I Was a Revolutionary*

SIN EATERS

SIN EATERS

STORIES

CALEB TANKERSLEY

University of Alaska Press
Fairbanks

© 2022 by University Press of Colorado

Published by University of Alaska Press
An imprint of University Press of Colorado
245 Century Circle, Suite 202
Louisville, Colorado 80027

Cover photo by Ian Dooley, https://unsplash.com/photos/v9sAFGJ3Ojk.
Cover and interior design by Krista West.

 The University Press of Colorado is a proud member of the
Association of University Presses.

The University Press of Colorado is a cooperative publishing enterprise sup-
ported, in part, by Adams State University, Colorado State University, Fort Lewis
College, Metropolitan State University of Denver, University of Alaska, University
of Colorado, University of Northern Colorado, University of Wyoming, Utah State
University, and Western Colorado University.

∞ This paper meets the requirements of the ANSI/NISO Z39.48-1992
(Permanence of Paper).

ISBN: 978-1-60223-451-2 (paperback)
ISBN: 978-1-60223-452-9 (ebook)
https://doi.org/10.5876/9781602234529

Cataloging-in-Publication data for this title is available online at the
Library of Congress.

For Richie—magpakailanman

The devil can cite Scripture for his purpose.
An evil soul producing holy witness
Is like a villain with a smiling cheek,
A goodly apple rotten at the heart.

—Shakespeare, *The Merchant of Venice*

✠

I would rather be wrong
than live in the shadows of your song

—Arcade Fire

CONTENTS

SWAMP CREATURES

While we're eating dinner or when we're tired of fighting, my husband and I stare at the swamp behind our house. Gary sips beer as he watches the festering water with awe, like an important piece of architecture. "How far down does it go? Fifty feet? Do you think?" He asks and answers his own question before spearing a chunk of beef and swallowing it whole. I grill steaks every Thursday, cook them just right with little bits of juice and blood pooling on the plate. Gary never pauses to taste his food, always slops it in. Like it's all the same.

The swamp is impressive, a gargling pool stretching as far as we can see from our backyard, tall ghostly trees sticking out of it and obscuring the horizon. We've been renting the same house two years but never explore too far back, some sense of reverence holding us.

It's been three months since I lost my job at the dry cleaners. Business was down, they said. Nothing personal. I just wasn't needed. Gary works computers for a bank, stays inside all day. But he likes to pretend it's back-breaking labor. He comes in, takes off his pants, and falls on the couch with a big sigh. "Another day, another dollar."

The swamp is like a bustling kingdom, so many different animals. Dragonflies, timid snakes, hundreds of tiny fish darting around like little bits of cellophane, gutsy but barely there. Bubbles stream up to the surface of the swamp, sometimes in one spot, other times forming trails. "I bet there's some kind of creature down there. We're too far north for gators, aren't we? Do you think?" I've got in the habit of ignoring Gary's questions. He doesn't seem to notice.

I spend most of my days watching movies in bed. We have a big flat screen in the living room, but the couch and entertainment center feel more like Gary's. His smell is on them. Years ago I loved that smell, used to crumple his clothes to my nose when he was away. But time melts the view of people you love, like leaving a painting out in the rain.

I prefer black and white movies. The classic feel. I watch detective stories, narrow my eyes and hold a pen to my mouth like I'm smoking. I want to be Humphrey Bogart's "dame."

I call my sister Amy every afternoon. The calls would be unbearable if she were happy, if her marriage was wonderful but thankfully she hates her husband too. Donny. We talk about laundry, what's on sale, our old friends from high school, mostly the ones doing worse than us. But I keep circling back to the swamp. "Yesterday I watched two snapping turtles fighting. Each one was bigger than my head. You wouldn't think it about turtles but their fins have these massive claws. For three hours they struggled until they were covered in blood and muck. Eventually one dove and never came back up. It was so brutal. And exhilarating."

"Karen, you can't keep doing this to yourself," Her kids are screaming and running in the background. "You need more in your life." It's never occurred to me that what I have isn't enough, doesn't constitute an existence. I turn up the volume on the TV.

I met Gary when I was sixteen and he was twenty-two. My mother had just died from a tumor along her spine. She was traditional, never used a microwave and didn't believe in modern medicine, in the weakness of pain meds. She spent an entire winter in bed, moaning constantly, the small knot in her back growing from a raisin to a cherry to a lime to an apple, a giant lump, hard as rock and covered in thick purple veins. It took Mom months to die, long enough for this lump to break her, become her. Of course I cried for days, but as soon as the last shovel of dirt fell on her grave, my tears dried up. I walked the streets of our neighborhood at dusk, stopped at the first house party, drank the first beer hand-ed to me, said yes to the first boy.

I often sit out by the swamp in the hottest part of the day. There's a smell to it, musty, rank, and satisfying all at once. A post-sex smell. At first I didn't like it, was out there to offend my own senses. But after a few weeks I thought about that smell all the time, especially when Gary was on top of me. Gary never calls it sex, always "making love." When we do it I can always tell by the way he scrunches his face that it's not going to take him very long.

The swamp has so much to offer if you're willing to wait.

Gary comes home and asks again if we can have a baby. I'm in bed knitting and watching *The Creature from the Black Lagoon*, my favorite movie. The black and white makes everything look harsh and sharp as rocks.

"We could name him after me. Or her after you. Whichever." The creature's eyes are bright against its dark slimy skin, fangs pulled out as it watches a woman swimming from below. I adjust the sleeves on the sweater I'm knitting. I've made it too small for Gary but I'm knitting it anyway.

"You'd have someone to keep you company. While you're here." I can't remember him ever wearing a sweater, which seems weird, to never wear a sweater. "Or we could adopt. Some little girl from a troubled home. I've always wanted a little girl. Don't you think we'd make great parents? Believe you me I'd raise her right."

I keep knitting as I watch the creature, fish lips open, webbed claws extending toward the woman. She doesn't know. The crea-ture swims next to her now, just beneath where she can't see. The music rises dramatically. "I used to love you." I say it without mov-ing my face from the screen.

Gary puts his hands in his pockets, gives the bedpost a light tap with his foot. "I know."

I'm not surprised he knows, just surprised he would say it. We rarely show our real selves. I work hard not to look at him.

"Just think about the baby." He leaves the room.

I have a dream about the creature from the black lagoon. It's swimming beneath me and of course I enjoy it. Then I dream about my mother. At first she's herself, the mother I knew when I was five. Then it's only my mother's tumor, a sack of throbbing skin that never stops growing, now larger than our house, now covering the horizon. I ask myself Gary's question: How far down does it go?

"I want you to talk to somebody," Amy says.

I take a small bite out of a piece of toast, tear off small chunks and toss them to the fish. The way they twist and curl is so elegant, like following the strokes of a clock. "We're talking right now."

"You know what I mean." I hear dishes clanging. Amy's good at house stuff. My counter is full of old pots that are starting to stink.

"I wouldn't know what to say."

"You know you don't have to be unhappy, right? You could do something else. Find someone else." She's scrubbing so hard I can hear it through the phone. "I want you to be happy, okay?"

"I know." The fish scatter as a giant turtle pops up. He bobs and looks at me. We watch each other for a while. I've only taken that one bite, but I throw in the rest of the toast, watch as the turtle jabs at it, his beak striking so fast you can hardly see his neck extend three times its normal length. I could stand here forever, watching this turtle eat. That would make me happy.

"Hey, Karen, can you tell me again how to get wine stains out of silk?"

When we get off the phone I don't go back inside, keep standing by the swamp. If I slipped I could slide right in, right under. A log drifts far off next to one of the tall, white trees. The log's covered in moss so it looks like an alligator. It might be an alligator, but I won't tell Gary about it. There are so many noises coming from the swamp but I have no idea what they are.

The sun's gone down by the time Gary comes home. Or maybe he's been home for a few hours but he waited to come out behind the house and get me. I haven't moved, even though I really need to pee. It's just so peaceful. Part of me thinks if I don't move, if I stop and listen I really could stay here forever.

He walks down and stands next to me, doesn't talk. He's drinking a beer, offers it to me then pulls it back when I do nothing. Every once in a while Gary knows what to do, or at least what not to do. It makes me think of all the times when he was caring and charming. But they're old memories now, turned like soured milk. My stomach rumbles and I taste acid in my throat.

"We have a guest coming over."

I can't remember the last time we had anybody over. Amy and Donny maybe six months ago. "Who and when?"

Gary shuffles his feet. "You know Murray from work? He takes his kid to a Lutheran preschool. They're closed tomorrow for some religious holiday. He didn't know what to do, so I said she could stay here for the day. With you."

I grab the beer from Gary's fingers, take several gulps.

"Look, it's helping out a friend. And it might be good for you, for both of us to get some practice, don't you think? In case we want to have that baby."

"How old is she?"

Gary looks back at the house. "Five."

"She should be in kindergarten."

"They decided to hold her back a year."

I look out at the swamp and can't see anything, no fish or snakes or tiny bugs breaking the surface. The water's a flat shell so pristine I could almost step out on it, take it at a run, shoot off into the dark. "What's her name?"

"Starla."

I finish the beer and hand the bottle back to Gary. "Okay."

"Wonderful. It'll be fun having a kid around for the day, right?"

Gary grins as I step back and into the house, grab the sweater I'm working on then go pee. I stay in the bathroom for two hours, knitting a section then ripping it out and knitting it again.

When Gary's asleep, I step out to the back porch and call Amy. She's in the bathtub, where she spends a lot of her evenings.

"What's up?"

"Are you glad you have children?"

Some kind of Depeche Mode music plays in the background. "They're the only real reason I get up in the morning. That and good whiskey, which I'm sipping now."

"Gary wants to have a baby." Amy doesn't respond. "If it's a boy we're naming it after him. A girl, I guess she'll be little me."

"Don't do that."

"You're happy with your kids, right?" I'm watching the swamp as I talk. Lightning bugs and all kinds of glowing things float around, a million tiny eyes shining out at me.

"A baby isn't a fucking Prozac pill. It would probably make things worse for you. Sure, you might enjoy a kid. But you wouldn't enjoy it with Gary."

"We're having a test-run tomorrow." My nails are getting long. I use them to pick at bits of wood sticking out of the porch. "Gary told his coworker I would watch this guy's daughter. He named her Starla. Gary never even asked me."

I hear Amy stand up from the tub. "Just leave him, Karen. It's time."

"And go where?" Off among the trees and the slipping water, I can see this enormous tapestry, all these animal lights like a pulsing map of stars. It's beautiful. "I think this swamp is the love of my life."

"Jesus." Amy hangs up. The swamp sings and chirps, deep and dark and full of heat. I'm at peace, but inside I can feel myself changing.

✠

Out of bed much earlier than normal, I fix my hair and put on real clothes, make myself presentable. Gary's slurping cereal for breakfast while I sit across from him and sip coffee. I'm knitting on that sweater. It's growing smaller and smaller. The doorbell rings. He stands up, looks slightly embarrassed. I don't move, keep looping those big needles in and out of the string, building something unusable.

Gary leaves the room, I hear muffled voices, fake laughter. He comes back in with a little girl. She's walking in front, Gary behind her, bent down and gently pushing her forward. "Karen, honey, this is Starla. Starla, this is Ms. Karen." Starla stands still with a disgusted look. Her hair is thin and blond, done up in two pigtails. My mother used to give me pigtails. I didn't think kids got pigtails anymore. Starla wears a white shirt and bright pink pants, shoes with cartoon flowers on the sides.

"Hi." Starla gives me a blank stare. She's a big girl, round and surprisingly tall for five, comes up to Gary's waist.

"Hi, Starla." I meet her stare but keep knitting. I'm getting very good at setting my body off on its own path.

Gary pats Starla on the shoulder, smiles at her. "I'm sure you'll both have fun today. I have to go to work." He walks over to me, leans his face toward mine. We almost bump foreheads before I realize what this is, that he's trying to kiss me, pretend we're this blissfully married couple, put on a big fucking show for a five-year-old girl. I want to jam a knitting needle through his eye, shove it in and hammer until it comes out the back of him. Instead I grab his cheeks, squeeze as hard as I can and push him away, give him a soft brush with the fingertips. Just enough to let the girl know I don't always want to kill him. Gary's surprised, stands and leaves in silence. Then it's just us, me and Starla.

I keep knitting the sweater, weaving needles over each other. I prefer wood ones over plastic. I love the sound they make clacking together. Starla seems to enjoy it too. She doesn't move, doesn't say anything. Just watches my fingers twirl faster than I really know what they're doing.

"You want some coffee?"

"No."

"Starla. Where did that name come from?"

She sniffs, looks around the room as if she expects someone else to jump in and answer. "I don't know."

"You can sit if you want."

Starla pulls out a chair, sits across the table, stares at me with her mouth open before looking out a window. I move the sweater around on my lap. The bottom four inches are missing but I hold it up. "Want to try this on?"

We drag a dining chair into the bathroom. Starla wriggles onto the seat, struggles to stand up. I steady her with a hand. She seems pleased. The sweater comes down over her. It's a multitude of colors, red on the left sleeve, yellow on the collar, bright green near the bottom. I kept switching yarns, never bothered to start over. The collar is too wide, drags down her back, but the sleeves fit surprisingly well with her little fingers just sticking out from the ends. If anything, the middle seems snug. She really is big for five. I have no idea how big a five-year-old should be.

"It's pretty." She twirls around and watches herself in the mirror. I see myself and grin like an idiot for no reason, almost say "hello." I don't know either of these people, the ones in the mirror. Starla almost falls off the chair, steadies herself and jumps down.

"Do you like marshmallows?" She asks and grabs my hand.

"Not really."

"I like the colored ones. Do you have any?"

"We might have some. Probably just white ones, though."

Starla looks down, gives me this exaggerated sigh. "That's okay. I'll eat the white ones." She lifts her head and smiles so wide it forces her eyes closed. "Please please please?" How dangerous. She knows how to be adorable.

"Okay. Let's eat marshmallows. Do you want to watch a movie?"

Starla throws up her hands. "Yes!"

"Have you seen *The Creature from the Black Lagoon*?"

✠

I've watched the film so many times, could repeat all the dialogue, know all my favorite parts by heart. I spend most of my time watching Starla, her tiny fingers delicately picking marshmallows from the bag and moving them to her open mouth, eyes never leaving the screen as she wipes her hand on the sweater before reaching into the bag for more.

I want to touch her, run my hands over her tiny arms, the bridge of her nose. I want to ask her questions: *Can you swim? Can you feel all the bones in your mother's back? Do you know how turtles move? Have you ever watched a tumor grow?* But the one that comes out is "Do you know what it means to be fired?"

She turns her head, annoyed. "No." She waits for me to explain.

"It's just like in a gun, how people say 'I fired a bullet.' It's being thrown very fast, somewhere far away."

Starla stares with no emotion. She's so intricate. I love watching her think, the mechanisms turning behind the skin of her face. "I don't want to be fired."

"Sometimes I do. Sometimes I think it'd be nice."

"Yeah." She turns back to the TV, shoves three marshmallows into her mouth. We're watching on the big screen in the living room but it doesn't feel like Gary's room with Starla here.

The brass crescendos. A hand reaches from the water, sharp claws with webbed plates. Starla goes stiff and I worry about her choking on the marshmallows. It was an urban legend when I was young, some stupid kid in the neighborhood who died from too many marshmallows jammed down his throat.

Starla makes a little whimpering sound as the creature moves toward a tent. The occupants notice but it's too late. Gills contract around its face as the creature bellows like a dying bull, shoves its large claw over the faces of its victims. It's not clear whether they suffocate or their heads are ripped off. The movie leaves it to the imagination which is why I love the swamp so much, this enormous veil of water hiding the intricate lives of its creatures, the surface dotted with little impressions hinting at all that brilliance below.

Starla puts her hands over her ears, closes her eyes and starts screaming. Two marshmallows come flying out of her mouth. I don't know where the third has gone. Her scream climbs until its bouncing off the ceiling, filling the whole room. I don't know how to calm her down. "Jesus. Stop it. Just stop it."

She gets up and runs out the sliding door to the back porch. I can hear the sweater swishing with every little stride. It's a good minute or so before I collect myself, decide to follow. So much for babies.

✠

There are creatures in the swamp you learn to stay away from. Snakes with pointed heads or the old crawdads with bodies big and fat as apples, that bright little strip of blue on the edge of the claw. I'm not concerned when I first get up from the couch, but so many scenarios move through my brain—scenes with these creatures or possible alligators—by the time I reach the back porch that I'm moving faster and surprising myself with how worried I am. Maybe I could be some kind of mother.

It's strange how quiet it is, how the swamp reverberates my panic back at me when I step out on the porch and find the most normal scene. Nothing. No snakes or crawdads. No alligators. No Starla. She's just gone.

I start to say her name. It feels wrong but I keep saying it, louder and louder. Walking around the porch, the front and back yard, the swamp. I'm scanning for the sweater, a tiny scrap of colorful string that could lead me to wherever she's hiding. Or been taken. Only now do all the possibilities flood into me.

Every time I watch *The Creature from the Black Lagoon*, I observe new details that change the way I think. Before Starla screamed I noticed how gently the creature moved its webbed hands, placed them over its victim's mouth as if to whisper "I'm here now. It's okay." Walking the swamps—screaming, even reaching in and feeling around—a story takes shape, the Creature looking in from the window, watching us watching him in glorious black and white. He sees little Starla, sees her run away, moves his soft paw over her mouth—"I'm here now. It's okay."—before diving with her somewhere deep and safe.

When I was a little girl I liked to hide from my mother in department stores. I'd hunker down in the middle of a rack of shirts and stifle my laughter as I heard my mother run around, desperately calling my name. One time I waited too long. I could hear the manager and all kinds of employees looking for me. When I finally emerged my mother slapped me, right there in the store, in front of everyone. I remember in that moment wishing my mother was dead, and of course a few years later she was.

After searching everywhere I can think of, I go stand out by the swamp, the edges of my toes sticking into the water. I'm covered in leaves and mud, like I'm part of this now. A tick crawls up my forearm but I don't brush it off. If I wait, I hope the swamp will let me know, give me a sign. If I can only stand still. Disappear enough to see into things.

I don't know how much time passes before Gary comes home, steps out on the back porch. I've heard nothing from Starla but I'm starting to believe it, the story of the creature taking her to a place where she can find a better name.

Gary races around the yard then comes back and shakes my shoulders, spit flying out his mouth. He keeps asking questions but I don't respond. I've turned the volume down on Gary, his lips moving so fast with no sound to them. I'm outside of sound. I push him aside and without hesitation step into the swamp. We've been waiting for this a long time, the swamp and me. I sink straight away, my whole body immediately under. I'm surrounded by mud and can't even feel a bottom. It disturbs me to think that this much Gary may have got right. My god, how far down does it go? I come up, hover my nose over the surface and breathe in the smell. Gary's splashing behind me but I'm moving away from the shore. I'm drinking in big heaping gulps. Something keeps scraping my legs, twigs or tiny fish, but I'm hoping its them, the creature and Starla. They're waiting for me, just below the surface. I'm not moving my lips but I'm talking so fast, communicating like an animal, telling the creature "I'm here now. It's okay. Take me down."

CANDY CIGARETTES

The idea was to walk into every room as if the space itself were beneath her, already her own. This was how Mellie entered the shack behind the garage, each step resolute on the cold concrete. How to enter had been a good lesson. She scanned around, disapproved of what she saw. Like Grandpa always did. His smell lingered, cinnamon and engine oil. Wood shavings from his carpentry. The shack echoed empty without him, but Mellie liked to sit in his old chair and think, rework all the lessons he taught her.

Every afternoon before Grandpa died, Mellie ran into Grandpa's shack for training. She loved these lessons, thought about them constantly as she squirmed in her desk at school. The trainings were different each day, exercises Grandpa said would make her "ready to face the goddamn world." They'd been close, spent all their time together: chewing toothpicks, playing table tennis, or telling war stories, which Mellie enjoyed inventing. Even the hurried way they ate seemed shared, how Mom would yell at both of them for stuffing their mouths. Mom called Mellie Grandpa's shadow, an image that thrilled her. Grandpa told Mellie she was a special kid, that she had "ice-water veins." She didn't fully know what Grandpa meant, but she desperately wanted to prove him right.

Mellie rubbed her hands along the chair, lifted her fingers to find the prints laced with dust.

Without Grandpa, Mellie tried to train herself by stalking around the house, learning which steps didn't creak, listening in on conversations, a peek into that elusive adult world. She decided to sneak to her sister Janice's room. Spying on Janice was usually dull and easy, not much for training. But Mellie was bored deep in her bones. Ever since Grandpa died, Mellie had been waking up less interested in the day. Everything was losing its color.

Mellie left the shack, crept into the house, and climbed the stairs without a sound. The static of her own brain hissed in Mellie's ears, but Grandpa taught her not to distract herself, to tune it out. Janice's door was usually locked, but Mellie tried the knob. The cold metal didn't budge. Mellie pulled a Bobby pin from her hair. She wore a Bobby pin even when she didn't need it. The lock made a soft click. Mellie opened the door a few inches, just enough to see.

Janice had a friend over, Tracee who was really tall, taller than most of the boys. Tracee had long hair she wore straight and back, the hair reaching all the way down to her thighs. Mellie thought the long hair made Tracee look even taller. But everyone looked tall to Mellie. She was small for nine.

The thing that struck Mellie about peeking in Janice's room was the absence of height. Mellie looked up for a split second, expected Tracee there and found nothing. Adjusting her angles, she found only air and little particles of dust twisting in the sunlight coming through the window. Mellie's eyes followed the sunlight down to Tracee, laid out flat on the bed. Some of her clothes were off, but Mellie couldn't quite see Tracee's body. Janice was in the way.

Tracee made a yelp when she noticed Mellie spying. Janice leapt up, shoved the door closed. But Mellie could see before she was forced back that Tracee hadn't moved, enjoying what was happening to her even after it had stopped.

Mellie went back to her room and opened an old coloring book. She colored all the time, even though her mom never bought new coloring books. Mellie would scratch over what she'd already done, running blue crayons over yellow areas to make new colors that looked sometimes interesting and sometimes splotchy. She needed time to think about what would happen when Janice came into her room. Mellie needed to consider what she wanted.

✠

Every day since Grandpa died Mellie had dragged her feet down the hallways at school, her sneakers leaving gray streaks on the tile. A month without training days in the shack—running through the lessons, listening to Johnny Cash on scratched cassette tapes, Grandpa carving blocks of wood into strange animals or slingshots—left her feeling hollow. No more ice water pouring through her veins.

But this morning had been different, fresh and exciting. During the science lesson, Mrs. London, told the class all about eyes. Rods and cones. Colors, corneas, and pupils. The projector screen was filled with gross pictures that made Mellie squirm, close-ups of sliced eyeballs. Then Mrs. London paused, walked over to the door, and flipped the lights off. Mellie had sat up at that, something unusual, the pale sunlight coming from the windows just enough to see. "Everyone, find a partner and look into their eyes." Mellie sat for a moment. It was such a strange request. By the time she turned around everyone already had an eye partner. The only person left nearby was the desk in front of hers, Ronnie. Mellie never noticed boys, had never talked to Ronnie before. They didn't discuss being partners, just found each other and stared. Ronnie had dark eyes, the irises such a deep brown they almost melted into the pupil. But after gazing long enough, Mellie could see it, the rich amber color, the way the little strands grew lighter on the outside, the intricate folds. It was all so complicated, hidden in the little moons of Ronnie's face. Mrs. London flipped the lights on without warning. Ronnie's eye—she could only really focus on one, the left—sunk somehow, faster than Mellie could track. Some of the students gasped when the lights returned. The class quickly adjusted and faced front, embarrassed by the intimacy of observing each other so closely. But Mellie held her stare after Ronnie turned around. She couldn't stop watching him, didn't know why. Mellie wanted to say something to make Ronnie turn so she could see his eyes again. But the day ended without Ronnie acknowledging her at all.

Something about this morning—glimpsing Ronnie's beautiful eyes and then being ignored, rejected, silently challenged—woke Mellie up. For a moment, she remembered her training, the lessons forged from hard work in the shack. She wouldn't fail him. She would take what she wanted, like Grandpa. She would face the goddamn world.

✠

Grandpa believed people good at poker were good at life. He gave her lessons in the cards, flushes and pairs, what beat what, how to shuffle and deal like a pro. But mostly the training was on keeping your face still. Grandpa would bend down close, his wrinkled skin inches from hers, and say as many crazy things as he could think of. Mellie was supposed to not twitch a muscle. "I killed a dog today. Cute little Doberman. Beat his brains out with a shovel. What do you think of that? Want me to show him to you? There's a boatload of ice cream in the freezer with your name on it. Rocky rocky road. You want some? You do don't you. Well your mother won't let you have any. She's real mean. The other night she told me I was a useless old turd. You know you're my least favorite grandkid, don't you? You're my least favorite. Or maybe you're my favorite. Yeah, I think that's the one. Favorite." Grandpa would stop talking and move his face, make it funny and then angry, so angry his skin turned red and he looked like he might explode. Mellie had cracked some early on. But after a few weeks she got good, never flinched or reacted at all. The trick was to not look into Grandpa's eyes.

✠

Mellie was sifting through her 64-count crayon box for the right shades of yellow and brown. Janice usually stomped around the house, door handles flying open and denting the dry wall. But this time she tapped three times gently, stepped in with her head down. That's no way to enter a room, Mellie thought. Janice was taking the humble route. Mellie had expected yelling. Instead, her sister had the posture of a submissive animal. This thing—whatever it was with Janice and Tracee—was important to Janice. She looked terrified.

Janice's long hair fell around her face. Mellie just noticed Janice wore her hair the same way as Tracee. She'd been doing that for a while. "What did you see, Mel?"

Janice's eyes were mostly pale green with bits of amber. She shifted her weight, crossed her arms and waited for an answer. Having found the right shade of brown, Mellie turned back to her coloring, began to scribble. "I saw you with Tracee."

"What about me with Tracee?"

Mellie put down the crayon and faced Janice. She stilled her jaw, just like Grandpa. "You were doing things to her. Things she liked."

Janice blinked six times before responding. "What do you want? To not tell."

The question Mellie anticipated. Anticipating maneuvers had been another of Grandpa's lessons. The wise thinker was always ready and waiting. Except Mellie didn't know what she wanted. She wanted so many things. Chocolate oranges. A 128-count box of crayons. That poker set her mom wouldn't buy. Ronnie to smile at her. Ginger back from the shelter. Grandpa to live again. Dad to show up when he said he would. A big beautiful pool. Janice happier. A put together world.

Mellie distilled these thoughts into one concentrated mass and blurted out the first thing that fizzled to the top of her brain. "Candy cigarettes."

Janice narrowed her eyes. "What?"

"I want a lot of them. Three full cartons."

"Those sugar stick things?"

"Yes."

"Do they still make those? And do they actually come in cartons?"

"Why don't we ask Tracee. Or better yet, let's ask Mom." Mellie stared her sister down. Janice's mouth tightened to a thin rope.

"You'll get your damn candy."

"Tomorrow, please," Mellie smiled.

"Okay." Janice let out a breath and brushed back her hair. "Tomorrow." The door slammed as she left. There was the anger Mellie had expected. She could feel Janice move down the stairs and through the house. Janice was always loud on the stairs. Mellie went to the window, watched her sister leap into her blue beat-up Neon. Tracee came out taking small, hesitant steps. She turned to the house, to Mellie, and they held each other's faces for a while. But Tracee was too far away to see eye color. She slid into the passenger's side, and Janice took off. Mellie hoped her sister would go try to find some candy cigarettes and be back before Mom got home.

Mellie sat back on the floor, lay herself out over the coloring books and crayons, watched the ceiling and imagined what was behind it. And whatever might be behind the sky. She put a hand up to touch it. Grandpa would be proud.

✠

Along with face exercises and poker games, Grandpa gave Mellie a series of mantras. He'd teach her a phrase, and then they'd shout it back and forth until they were both hoarse and exhausted. Grandpa would have them sit in chairs across from each other, lean into Mellie's face and scream, "I am not an animal!" He'd look panting and desperate, like an animal. She always thought that was funny. But she never told him, never flinched a cheekbone.

"I am not an animal!" she yelled back. Sometimes she ended it with a high-pitched squeal, a sound only a little girl could make. Grandpa nodded at that, Mellie playing to her advantages.

"I control my desires. They do not control me!"

"I control my desires. They do not control me!"

"I find what I want and I take it!"

"I find what I want and I take it!"

When the mantras were over Grandpa would sit back and sigh. "You're ready to face the goddamn world." Then he would open a rusty drawer and pull out a box of candy cigarettes. Mellie didn't know where he got them. She never saw Grandpa go to the store. But the candy was always there. "They say these aren't good for kiddos anymore. Horseshit, that's what I say. Here," he handed her a single white piece. Mellie held it to her face, examined it like a diamond. "Don't go telling your mother."

✠

Janice returned five minutes before Mom got home. Tracee wasn't with her. Mom walked in and chewed Janice out for not having dinner started. As the pasta churned in the boiling water, Mellie asked Mom, "Where is Grandpa now?"

"Heaven, baby girl."

"Okay, but where is Heaven?"

Mom shrugged. "You know where. Up beyond the sky."

"But Mrs. London told us it was all darkness and dead stars up there."

"Go get your sister."

Mellie wondered if this was what Grandpa had always been preparing her for, if all the training and the exercises and the obstacle courses were about what happened when you died, if the world she was meant to face was where Grandpa was now, floating through an infinite cold nothing. Maybe Grandpa was training for himself too. He could be up there now, struggling. The thought almost made her cry.

When she opened Janice's door she was pleased to see two small boxes, each the size of a pack of cards and decorated in kitschy designs, horses and cowboys and sunsets.

"These weren't easy to find on short notice." Janice sat on her bed smoking a real one, the end sizzling to life.

Mellie glanced at the boxes. "You'll need more."

"I ordered more online. It'll take a day or two. In the meantime, you got these. When your cartons come in we're square?"

Mellie wrapped her fingers around both packs. "We will be."

Janice's shoulders fell as she exhaled. Mellie looked her sister up and down, as if for the first mysterious time. They watched each other until Janice shifted, folded her arms. "Fucking knock next time."

"Lock your door better. Dinner's ready."

Janice puffed more smoke out her nostrils. Mellie didn't want to admit it looked cool. "Spaghetti's not dinner."

"Tonight it is."

"Why are you such a fuck of a sister?"

Mellie relaxed her facial muscles, kept her eyes straight. Like Grandpa taught her. "I know how to face the goddamn world."

Janice fell back and laughed, her body shaking so that she put a hand over her stomach. Mellie shuffled out, taking the cartons with her.

"Don't let Mom see those!" Janice yelled through the door.

That night Mellie held the packs like jewels, kept them close as she slept, the candy within like her own precious clutch of eggs.

✠

Another lesson involved Grandpa pretending he didn't know Mellie, like they were strangers. Grandpa played this game without warning. On those days Mellie would walk in and see Grandpa standing in the middle of the shack, his eyes darting about the room in random order. Sometimes Grandpa looked like he was in pain, his fingers clasping and unclasping, all the scraps of wood and papers around his shack in disarray. Mellie would jump up and down, repeat her name. "Grandpa, it's Mellie! Mellie! I'm Mellie don't you know Mellie?"

Grandpa would squint his eyes and gasp for air. "What? Who? I don't know a Mellie."

"Your granddaughter!"

"Granddaughter? No, you must mean Mellie O'Neal from down the hill. You're in my brother's grade."

"No, I'm Mellie! Sharon's daughter? Your daughter named Sharon? She's my mom!"

Mellie would yell for what felt like hours. She would tell stories about their lives: the last time they ate ice cream, how Janice took an hour to get ready in their only bathroom. All the lessons and mantras they'd been through in the shack. After Mellie ran out of real stories she made them up: Mellie and Grandpa built their own submarine, explored sea creatures in the Mariana Trench. Mellie and Grandpa became detectives, only they got bored and turned bad, put on black masks and started robbing banks, running out the building with burlap sacks full of cash. Mellie and Grandpa lived together at the North Pole. They knew there wasn't a real Santa Claus, but they decided there should be. They built a giant factory, started making dolls and rocking horses in the frozen north.

Eventually Grandpa's skin turned ghostly white. Then he'd sit in his chair, his breath relaxing and his fingers releasing their tension before patting her on the head. "Well done, kiddo. You came in after me. And you never gave up. That's the secret. This is a test, for stamina. But sometime later I might actually forget you. When that happens, you've got to stay calm and come in after me."

The memory lesson scared her, how it went on for so long, like Grandpa's body was nothing but a pasty husk. She questioned what really occurred during the lesson, whether Grandpa pretended or whether it was actually happening, if he had forgotten her. She hated screaming at Grandpa until tears ran down both their chins. But he always smiled and gave her a big bearhug when she passed. Grandpa opened the bottom drawer of his desk, a metal screech jarring the air. He placed an entire pack of candy cigarettes on her outstretched palm. "Don't go nuts."

✠

The next morning, Mellie woke up and crept into Janice's room. Janice looked so peaceful when she slept, like a completely different person, her eyes moving quickly under her lids. Mellie didn't want to wake her, but when she reached the foot of the bed Janice's eyes opened immediately, like pressing a button.

"What?"

Mellie didn't have a response ready, decided silence was best.

"I told you, you'll get the rest whenever the box shows up. Today or tomorrow. Chill out."

Mellie backed up to the door. Before leaving the room she whispered, "Tell Tracee I said hi." She wanted to get back at Janice for laughing last night, but as Janice's forehead crumpled and her eyes watered, Mellie regretted her words. Janice should have listened to Grandpa, Mellie thought. She should learn to control her face muscles. Mellie closed the door, hurried into the bathroom to prepare for school.

Stepping past lockers in the hallway, Mellie's whole body shook with electricity, like she could explode or melt at any moment. In her pocket were two whole packs of candy cigarettes. She hadn't eaten a stick, hadn't even opened the boxes. Mellie laid awake half the night, watching the ceiling and talking to Grandpa out there in the void. She needed his help planning, anticipating. How to use this new variable to her advantage.

This was the first morning since Grandpa died that Mellie had woken up thrilled to be alive, each breath a small surprise. At night she felt herself nearer to Grandpa, somewhere in the sky or the ground or the land of the dead. But now—with Ronnie—she had a real purpose again in the living world. Planning and strategizing were Grandpa's best skills. In her dreams they worked it out together, as if he'd never left.

Mellie walked into her classroom, right past Ronnie's desk, and didn't look at him. She'd coerced Janice into helping her with her hair today, a little curl to the bottom shaping just below her cheeks. Mellie could feel the curls bouncing as she walked by, and she knew it looked good. She wanted to see him see her, but Grandpa had taught her well. So very well. She never twitched her neck Ronnie's way, sat at her desk and studied the back of his head, his hair a deep gorgeous brown, a few invisible strands standing up toward the light.

Social Studies, Math, Reading, and then lunch. Mellie just had to make it to lunch. The hours were grueling, and she could barely pay attention. Her eyes kept drifting to the window, staring at nothing but thin clouds. So much so that Mrs. London scolded her in front of the class: "Please keep your brain here today." Mellie smirked to herself. The extra attention would help.

At the lunch bell, Mellie ran into the cafeteria. She found a spot just inside the door, next to the plastic barrel trash can. All the other kids filed in through the same entrance. She leaned against the wall with her arms crossed, narrowed her eyes. When Ronnie came in she called to him, "Hey! Ron." and beckoned him over. Ronnie looked confused, but stepped over by the trash can.

"My name is Ronnie."

"Yeah, I know." Mellie saw herself from Ronnie's view, her relaxed stance, her casual eyes. "You ever seen one of these?" Mellie held up the box, the one with the cowboy.

"No." Ronnie shifted his weight from right to left.

"They're called candy cigarettes. Shaped like cigarettes, but delicious candy." Mellie leaned in toward Ronnie's deep brown pools, the colors changing with the angle of the light. "Want one?"

Ronnie looked around. He reached a long, slender finger up to scratch the side of his head. Up close, he was even more beautiful. "I guess."

"Here." Mellie popped open the box.

The cigarettes inside were small, their textures pocked and grainy. They should have looked a brilliant white, but these cigarettes were slightly yellowed. She made a mental note to complain to Janice later about buying the cheap brand, maybe guilt her into buying double. Mellie placed a single cigarette on Ronnie's palm.

"What is this?"

"Give it a whirl, Ron. You'll love it." Mellie leaned farther back on the wall and gave Ronnie a wink. Ronnie hesitated, briefly sniffed the cigarette before placing it in his mouth.

A good candy cigarette is a thing of beauty, the sound crisp and bright when snapped. But when Ronnie bit down all Mellie heard was a moist splat. The cigarette bent rather than broke, some tiny drop of liquid leaking into Ronnie's mouth. He spewed the candy onto the ground then stomped on it, but the cigarette refused to break up, instead smearing like melted wax.

"Gross! This tastes like mold."

Mellie leapt out of her stance, bent down and looked at the cigarette. "When my grandpa gave them to me they were always good."

Ronnie scraped his nails over his tongue. "Ugh, I can't get that taste out of my mouth. And that pukey smell. Thanks for nothing, smelly Mellie." Ronnie stomped on the yellow cigarette one more time before backing away. "Smelly Mellie! Smelly Mellie!" He chanted it louder, kids nearby joining in, laughing and pointing their fingers. Mellie backed against the wall, Grandpa's plan evaporating before her eyes. A few more chants went up before Mrs. London stepped into the cafeteria, and the taunting quickly died.

Although it seemed so stunningly obvious to her at that moment—that this would be her main insult through the rest of her life at school—Mellie had never been called a name before, let alone Smelly Mellie. She was not a girl who was normally noticed at all. To be teased was a new and devastating sensation. Grandpa taught her to anticipate, to know how the world worked and to take what she wanted. But as Ronnie joined the lunch line, smirking back at her and mouthing her new name to his friends, Mellie fell to her knees there by the trash can, crushed by the weight of having failed Grandpa so miserably.

✠

Mellie opened the door to the shack, the air filled with the hum of an old refrigerator and the smell of sawdust. Grandpa sat in his chair, a single desk lamp lighting the room. He stood and opened the freezer door, pulled out a tray of ice. "Hold out your hands."

She'd been doing well lately, passing lessons, winning poker games and strengthening her mind. But Mellie dreaded the physical challenges, doing push-up or wall sits or jumping jacks until she threw up. Still, she had never backed down from a lesson before. With slow, measured movements, Mellie extended both hands in front of her.

"Ninety degrees." She straightened her arms. "Palms up." The hands turned.

Mellie drew in deep breaths. Grandpa bent down on one knee. "My Mellie. You know you're the bravest person I know? This," he popped the tray, "is nothing to you. You remember what you have? Ice-water veins. This isn't pain. These little cubes here. These are friends. They're no match for you."

Grandpa stood up and gingerly placed a single cube in each palm. It felt like nothing at first, a slight glow. Then the stinging spread out to Mellie's wrists, down the length of her fingers. Dull cold blossomed into sharp pain. She closed her eyes. Before had been tests of the mind, but this was something different, something that prevented her brain from forming a single continuous thought.

"Grandpa . . ."

"You want to drop them? You giving in to a few little shits of ice?"

"But, Grandpa—"

"What do you want?"

Mellie could barely think. Despite the ice, her arms felt like they were burning. A painful numbness washed over her. Mellie started to shiver, struggled to remain still. The cubes wobbled. Through it all, from somewhere inside, she found a voice. "I want to complete the lesson!"

"What do we say?"

"I control my desires, they do not control me!"

Grandpa stood back, watched her face. "Is that so? How about controlling this." Grandpa took another ice cube, settled it on Mellie's left forearm. Then one for the right, and two more for the shoulders. "Don't you dare let those fall. They have to melt all the way. Unless you do first." Grandpa smiled. "Now how do you feel?"

The cold was like every bad thought sweeping through her body, every lonely night, every worthless morning. But no matter how little feeling burned away, she held her arms. Mellie made slight movements and shifts in balance to keep the ice cubes from running off with all the water pouring down. When she felt the cold in her bones she opened her eyes, pointed them right at Grandpa. "I'm ready to face the goddamn world."

"Is that so, little girl? What are you gonna do when you face it?"

"Take what I want!"

"Prove it."

By now the cubes in Mellie's palms were tiny stones, her arms drenched in freezing water. Although she could not feel her fingers, Mellie wrapped them around each small cube, brought them to her mouth, and swallowed. Her hands rolled out again, flat as the horizon. "I want more."

✠

Mellie didn't bother knocking on Janice's door, didn't feel she had to anymore. But when she walked in Janice wasn't there. It was only Tracee, hugging her knees to her chest on Janice's bed. Tracee had a strange face, elongated with bright skin. But she did have a nice smile, and when she saw Mellie in the doorway her lips pulled back, and she gave a small wave. "Looking for Janice?"

"Yep."

"She's out."

"Oh."

Tracee patted her hand on the bed. "You want to come and talk? About what you saw the other day?"

"Not with you."

Tracee's smile dropped. "I'm sorry about your Grandpa." They watched each other, held their stares again until they were interrupted by the sound of tires crunching gravel in their driveway. Mellie left Tracee and leapt down the stairs, met Janice as she opened the door. Although the floor was dirty, Janice wiped her boots on the rug. "Have a good smoke today?"

Mellie reached into her pocket, pulled out the box she'd shown to Ronnie and threw it at Janice's face.

"Shit!" The box struck Janice's chin before falling to her feet. "What was that about? I got you your damn candy."

"These are gross, stale, and unacceptable. They ruined everything! Where did you get this shit candy?"

Janice rubbed a hand over her face. "Where do you think I found candy cigarettes on short notice? There were a few old boxes on top of a bookcase in Grandpa's shack."

Mellie reached for the box she'd thrown, scooped it into her palm. "This is from Grandpa? You took these from Grandpa?"

"You wanted them right away. What was I supposed to do?"

Mellie stood up, pocketed the old cigarettes, and faced her sister. "Tonight I'm going to tell Mom." Janice's body went still like she'd stopped breathing. Then she backed up against the wall. Mellie expected more curses, but Janice only whispered, "Please, Mel . . . don't."

Moments like this were rare, Mellie so completely in control of a situation. She'd hoped to anticipate earlier with Ronnie, to be in control, but that had been a disaster. At least here, with something powerful over her sister, Mellie could relax. This was exactly what Grandpa trained her for. Mellie smiled. "Or maybe I'll go next door. I'll tell Mrs. Francis while she's out watering her Marigolds. What do you think she'll say?" Mellie took a step toward Janice. "Or I could tell Dad the next time he shows." Mellie took another step. "How many people do you want me to tell?"

Janice slid down the wall, her lips trembling as she squeezed her eyes shut. They were so close to each other, Janice's panicked breaths striking Mellie's cheek.

"Go on. Tell them." Tracee had come downstairs and stood straight in the middle of the living room.

Mellie moved toward Tracee. She loved how Tracee's face stayed still, her eyebrows low and harsh. Mellie hoped when she got older for harsh eyebrows. "Aren't you scared for everyone to know what you've done?"

Tracee stepped around Mellie, grabbed Janice's hand, and pulled her up. "I'm scared of a lot of things." Tracee seemed even taller than normal when she turned to Mellie. "You like to be tough. I get that. Really, though, what's so special about this candy? What's so important that you'd treat your sister like this?"

Janice and Tracee both watched her, waited for a real answer. Janice wiped her eyes then squeezed Tracee's hand.

Directness like this from Tracee was an outcome Mellie hadn't anticipated. She didn't know why she even bothered addressing these two who couldn't understand everything Grandpa helped her see. But something inside her had been coiled tight, chose this moment to break. Before Mellie realized what her lips were doing, she gave a truthful answer. "I control my own desires. That's what Grandpa wanted, for me to get what I want. And see, there's this boy who sits in front of me with beautiful eyes and fingers, Ronnie. I like him. Grandpa taught me to plan and anticipate so I could face the goddamn world, so I need the candy cigarettes to get Ronnie to like me."

Mellie expected them both to be proud. Here she was, younger yet more ambitious, pursuing her desires while they were afraid, hiding upstairs from the rest of the world. But for a long moment Janice and Tracee didn't say a thing.

Tracee broke the silence. "Jesus, kid," then gave Mellie a look that felt like her skin coming off, like Tracee could see to her bones.

Before Mellie could respond Tracee grabbed Janice's hand, leaned down and kissed her. Mellie had rarely seen anyone kiss in real life, and definitely not so close up with someone she knew. There was more sound than she'd expected. It felt strange, like she shouldn't be there. After their lips pulled away from each other they stayed close, fingers intertwined. Without moving her eyes from Janice, Tracee spoke to Mellie. "Go on then you little shit. Sell out your sister for old candy. That's really gonna bring the boys running. She and me, we'll be fine." Tracee kissed Janice one more time, and they were both quickly out the door, the living room suddenly silent as Mellie realized she'd lost yet another battle.

Mellie thought the cigarettes would impress Ronnie. She'd always felt so special when Grandpa gave them to her, cherished each one like a trophy as it dissolved on her tongue. But the cigarettes had backfired. She'd failed. Mellie imagined she held leverage over her sister, but Tracee had robbed her of this as well. All the training with Grandpa ruined. He was up there, in the black, watching her crumble.

Mellie stood by the front door for a minute. The old candy cigarettes began to feel clammy in her hand, the sour smell hitting her nose. She took them upstairs, laid them in the bottom of a drawer. Then she pulled out her coloring books, started inventing new ways of seeing.

Janice was back by the time Mom came home with a bucket of fried chicken. All three of them sat around the table, eating without talking. Janice took two bites of her food, barely lifted her head. Mostly she just picked at the chicken's skin with her fingers, peeling off little strips and bringing them up to her mouth.

Mom watched them both carefully. "Come on, girls. Chow down." Their mother finished a drumstick in three bites. Mellie thought Mom should compete, win a chicken-eating contest, use the money to buy them better food.

When their mother's mouth was full, Mellie tapped Janice under the table with her foot. Then Mellie spoke. "Hey, Mom?" Janice lifted her eyes, and they watched each other as their mother chewed, the silence interrupted by the shredding of greasy meat.

"Yeah?"

"Do you think Tracee's pretty?" Janice's whole body tensed. Mom said nothing, took another bite, and then quickly swallowed.

"Who?" Mom reached for another piece, this time the kind with breading stuck between little ribs.

"Tracee. Janice's tall friend. Don't you think she's pretty?" Janice lowered her head. A curtain of hair covered her face.

Mom shrugged. "No. Not really." They all three ceased chewing. The room froze for a moment before Janice stood up from the table, climbed the stairs.

Mom looked at Mellie. "I shouldn't have said that." She sucked on a bone before laying it down, a small pile to the right of her plate.

Mellie picked up a tiny bone. She couldn't tell by the shape where it should go. "Grandpa liked the leftover bones."

"He liked to eat the marrow inside. Slurped it out like crab meat."

Mellie looked down the length of her own arm, imagined Grandpa cracking her skin open, sucking out the middle of her bones. "Grandpa was kind of weird sometimes."

Mom picked clean her last tiny rib. "He sure was."

Mellie found Janice on the bed, her body in the same curled position Tracee's had been, another cigarette in her hand, smoke lazing its way out the window. Mellie ran a finger down the wood of the doorframe. "I didn't tell her."

"So you can blackmail me some other time?"

"I'm not going to tell her."

Janice leaned her head on the windowsill, watched the night sky. "Such a little saint."

In the moonlight Janice's face looked like stone, the lines carved deep into her cheeks. Mellie wanted Ronnie, sure, but she wanted Janice happy too. Mellie wanted too many things that ripped her apart, tore her flesh into little rolled strips.

Janice lay back on her bed, the cigarette pointing straight up at the ceiling. "There's a package for you on my dresser. Your fancy new cigarettes." Barely lifting her head, Janice locked eyes with her sister. "Thanks for not telling."

Mellie grabbed the box and ran out of the room before Janice changed her mind. Here was her second chance. This time she would catch Ronnie's eye. She would redeem them both, make Grandpa proud. It wouldn't be so bad for him up there, drifting between stars. Before going to bed Mellie decided to check. She opened a fresh box, smelled it and took a bite. The crunch echoed off the walls of her bedroom, and a sweetness settled on her tongue as she fell asleep.

✠

One day Mellie found Grandpa sitting in his chair, petting a little dog. She could already see it, what the training would be. Mellie took a step back, but Grandpa narrowed his eyes, He didn't even have to mouth the words, just give the look that said *don't you back down.*

The puppy was brown with little puffs of white on its side. Grandpa scratched it there with his massive hands like lobster claws. "Do you know what this little thing is made of?"

Mellie looked down at her own body. "Bones and Guts?"

The shack was dim, the way Grandpa liked it. It took her eyes time to adjust, to notice him smiling as he kept stroking the puppy's back. "Bones and Guts. A little shit thrown in for good measure. Here."

Mellie stepped forward, and Grandpa gave them to each other. As she pulled the puppy in close it wagged its tail and licked her cheek. "I'll call him Ginger."

"Her."

Mellie hugged Ginger, then dropped her face. Coldness swept her skin. Was this part of it? Giving her something to love and seeing if she'd let it go, hurt and break it? "What do you want me to do with it?"

Grandpa's eyes seemed watery, his skin pitted like rocks. He was suddenly old. "Take care of her."

Mellie set Ginger down on the concrete floor of the shack. Ginger whined and shivered. But Mellie stood up straight, looked ahead. She couldn't do this, love a puppy if Grandpa was going to make her do something cruel. She wanted it over with. "No games. No trick lessons. Tell me what to do."

Grandpa dropped from the chair, landed hard on his knees. It must have hurt, but he didn't make a sound, just scooped Ginger up in his arms. "We have games and lessons to make you strong. But some things are too precious for games. You need to know which are which. Now go get Ginger some chow. There's food for her in the kitchen. Your mom'll raise hell, but leave that to me."

Mellie still didn't trust—like he'd taught her—that this wasn't some elaborate lesson, but she lifted Ginger. She couldn't believe her luck, something so soft and loving, hers. When she left the shack Grandpa was still down on the floor, resting on his knees.

Three nights later Grandpa died in his sleep.

After the funeral, Mom came for Ginger. "It was your Grandpa's dog. Who's going to take care of her when everyone's gone all day?"

Mellie didn't cry at Grandpa's funeral. Holding back tears felt like her best tribute to him. But when Mom grabbed Ginger under her little brown paws Mellie raged in a hysterical way she hadn't done since she was five. Her body fell to the floor, neck arched and red, legs squirming like they were on fire. If she couldn't cry, at least she could shriek. Like an animal. "Grandpa gave Ginger to me! She's my dog! I take what I want from this world!"

Mom watched but didn't care, didn't react to anything Mellie did or said. Mom could hold back. She was good at it too. Probably from Grandpa. More than anything, she just looked tired. With Ginger in a cardboard box, Mom drove off to the shelter. As soon as the front door shut Mellie quit crying, lay on the carpet, calmed herself with deep breaths and watched the ceiling fan. *This was the greatest lesson of all.*

✠

The next day at school, Mellie bided her time. She didn't look at Ronnie or say anything, but during reading and Earth science and American history she bore a hole into the back of his head with her eyes, focused on him until her forehead was strained. He kept turning around, feeling her gaze. But she didn't divert. In her brain she kept the mantras going, one after the other. *I am not an animal. I control my desires, they do not control me. I take what I want from this world.*

At lunch Ronnie approached her, a small group of friends walking behind him. "What do you want with me, Smelly Mellie?" His friends snickered, but Mellie kept calm, took a drink of her milk carton before answering.

"Hey, Ron Ron. I dare you to try another candy cigarette. Meet me by the front doors after school. Unless you're a little shit."

Ronnie's friends gasped, danced around him laughing. "Whoa, did you hear that from Smelly Mellie?" She was upset the name had already spread around but didn't let it show.

Ronnie shifted his weight from foot to foot. "No, you're the little shit." He walked away, trailed by his friends. His only response was to parrot back at her. This meant he would show.

Mellie ran to the front doors after school. She wanted to arrive first, find a good position, but when she left the building Ronnie was already there. Half her class was with him, all circled around. She walked slow, paced with confidence. Grandpa's teaching coursed through her. She could feel the ice just beneath her skin. Mellie approached, and the circle of kids parted like a wave to let her in. Ronnie stood in the middle. "Here she is. Smelly Mellie."

"I thought you'd chicken out."

"What's this about? Do you want to give me more fart candy?"

"No fart candy. Just the good cigarettes this time." Mellie pulled out a box, this one featuring an eagle. The box was in the shape of a real pack of cigarettes, and the sight of it sent a murmur through the crowd. "Here, Ron Ron. Go nuts."

Ronnie snatched the box with his long fingers. Mellie couldn't help herself. She was still watching him. They'd been in a feud, but she never forgot how gorgeous he was, those brown eyes like swimming in chocolate sauce. Mellie saw their future together, the it couple of the school. Ronnie would love the candy cigarettes, all the kids would. She would not be Smelly Mellie but Candy Girl, the one with all the best sweet stuff, even the edgy ones, the cigarettes. They'd all become friends. Brush each other's hair and invite her to sleepovers. Ronnie would be her partner in crime. They'd start an underground trade, candy in exchange for Yo-Yos, Lunchables, answers to tests. They'd strut down the hallways hand in hand, candy cigarettes flayed out from all the spaces between their joined fingers. They would take what they wanted from this world.

Ronnie tore open the box, pulled out a white stick. The crowd looked at each other. His long fingers held the stick up, brought it close to his face. The smell of it—that pure white sweetness—floated over to Mellie. Ronnie bit down, and she could hear the clear snap of a quality candy cigarette. As he chewed, she crossed her arms and smiled at the sky. The class went quiet, leaned forward.

"This tastes like," Ronnie ran his tongue along the inside of his cheek, "nothing. It's grainy, maybe a little sweet. But mostly nothing. Old people candy."

Ronnie's friends broke the tension with cackles and screams. "Smelly Mellie and her grandma candy!" Taunting rose from the whole crowd.

"No, they're the best candy in the world! My Grandpa showed me—"

The laughter rose and drowned her response. Fingers pointed with more cheers. Ronnie egged them all on. "Smelly Mellie's a wrinkly old grandma! Here's what you do with old people candy!" He threw the entire box of cigarettes in the air. The crowd pounced on them with their shoes, grinding every one to powder, smeared into the grooves of the rippled concrete.

She thought the candy cigarettes had the power to make anybody feel special. That Ronnie would look at her the way she looked at him. That with planning would come control. Now none of it would ever happen, no sleepovers, no handholding, no Ronnie. She'd taken nothing from the world. Instead, she'd let the world take from her.

Mellie slinked off. Somewhere out there Grandpa was seeing this. The chants of "there goes Smelly Grandma Mellie" echoed out and up, to the milky dark heaven where Grandpa lived. She was glad he was gone so she didn't have to face him, tell him how she'd failed him all over again.

Mellie ran into the parking lot, scrunched down between cars. She could see herself clearly now, and she finally cried. Stupid girl. Pursuing Ronnie had been her sole focus. Now she felt empty, like a tired engine. What did she want now? It used to be so many things. But nothing was left to want.

"Hey." Wiping a hand across her chin, Mellie strained her neck to see Janice, long hair whipping behind her. "Mel, what's wrong?" Mellie's arms wrapped around her knees and hid her face. Her sister bent down, put a hand over Mellie's shoulder. "Is this about that boy? Ronnie?"

Mellie could feel a stream of snot falling from her left nostril. "Yeah."

"What happened?" Janice waited, but got no response. "It's okay. Boys are assholes sometimes. Most times."

Mellie looked into her sister's eyes. Pure, deep green, down into all the folds and lines stretching out like stems of grass. "Janice?"

"Yeah?"

"Mom was wrong. Tracee is very pretty."

"I think so too." Janice lifted her head to look behind her, then back at Mellie. "I've got an idea. Come on." Janice stood up, then offered her hand. Mellie wasn't used to help, especially from Janice. They mostly stayed away from each other. Mom barely noticed her. Dad showed up maybe twice a year. Grandpa used to intentionally knock her down so that she could learn to pick herself up. Sometimes he even held his hand over her, used his weight to press her, make Mellie fight to stand on her own. It was against all the lessons, all the mantras. But here, in the school parking lot, tears and snot running down her chin, Mellie accepted her sister's long, outstretched hand.

✠

Ronnie and his friends milled about the front doors when an old Neon pulled to the curb. The side was dented with blue paint chipping off, but it was the sort of weathered car they all dreamed of owning someday. So rough it was cool. A girl with green eyes and long hair rolled the window down, leaned out.

"Ronnie!" All the kids turned, not to the car but to Ronnie, who put his hand to his chest, giddy at being singled out by a mysterious high-school girl.

She pulled out a candy cigarette, held it up for the crowd to see, and placed it in her mouth. Janice snapped the cigarette in two so hard the sound reverberated off the school walls. After she chewed and swallowed she pointed her long arm straight at Ronnie. "Suck it, shitbag!"

Tracee moved her own head out the window, her face covered by large sunglasses and a cigarette dangling from her lips. "Go to hell, Ronnie!"

Mellie lifted her head out the backseat window. "Yeah, shitbag!"

The girls whooped, and the car peeled off down the street. Although no one was sure how badly he had been burned, everyone could sense Ronnie as the new pariah. They gave him a wide berth as they waited, backpacks in hand, for their parents to arrive and finally take them home.

HE TOLD ME A STORY

He had a hole in his chest the size of a grenade, of something I could have cupped in my palm. Tiny valleys slithered in and out of it, stretching from his armpit to just above a dark nipple. It collected beads of sweat like a trough. My fingers ran along the bottom, scraping the coarse skin dry. I licked every drop as he sat silent, looked away.

He told me a story about whiskey behind the wheel. About killing a father of three. About the hot pipe that seared him. About the dead man's wife, how her hand touched his gently, her smile curved above the scar that would become the hole. About her forgiveness. About cheapness and sweat.

I focused on the scar, the mesh of skin and space moving back and forth, closer and farther away. He liked it hard and angry, wanted his love to sear me. But then he'd cup my face in his palm, be gentle, surprise me.

APPARITIONS

Pulling the blankets off David, I twist them around my whole body until only my face sticks out between thick puffs of cloth. The blankets are green and filled with cotton so that I look like a fat caterpillar. I'm trying to be cute and agitate him, but David pretends he's impervious to the cold of the bedroom, sits up against the headboard and crosses his arms. "That doesn't work on me." He tries not to smile, fails.

"Sure. You're a real mountain man." Abandoning the blankets, I burst out and sit before he stands up next to the bed, stretches his body toward the ceiling. Three years together and no matter how much David eats he keeps getting thinner. I've been steadily gaining, my middle round and soft. David's never once complained. He's so much smaller than me now. His entire frame could fit inside my own, wear my ribcage like a vest.

A constant stack of magazines hangs by the bed. We rarely read them, but tonight I turn on a lamp and grab a *National Geographic* off the pile, flip through the pages. "Did you say yes to your boss about Cazadero?" I stretch the "z" longer than necessary. David's an accountant for a real estate conglomerate. Last week he was offered a transfer out of Birmingham to Cazadero, a small California town near the coast. I got excited, looked up the street view of shops and museums, picked out where we could live, where to get nice sushi on Fridays.

"I'm still considering." All of his family lives three hours away, and he loves Birmingham, says he'd miss the comfortable bars and driving past that massive Vulcan where we first kissed.

"I've got considerations for you: beaches and Democrats."

"Alright." David puts his hands up in surrender and backs to the door. He drops the stance and bounces around, boxing the air as he moves into the bathroom. I'm one article down when I hear the shower turn on, think about the cities and the trees and the dry California air.

A few minutes later he calls out for me. "Logan!" David comes back into the bedroom, drips water on the carpet, the fibers soggy and smashed in foot-shaped patterns from his steps. Used to he would have walked out in a towel, but for the last year David has been comfortable enough with me to be casually naked, droplets running from his hips down to his thighs.

He wipes water from his eyebrows. "Come look at the tub." Soap suds cling to his ears. We could shower together and I'd tell him "rinse your goddamn ears" and he'd still leave bubbles in the little crevices. Afterward I'd embrace him and hear the soft crinkling of foam.

Lying out on the bed, I glare over the glossy page, a feature on cockroaches of Madagascar. I'd hate to see David tangle with one of these things. He loves smashing bugs, gets a gleeful look in his eye every time a spider or cricket finds its way into our apartment. David always brings the squished remains to me for inspection. I try not to look.

"Whatever it is, baby, you're getting the carpet wet."

"I hate it when you call me baby. This isn't just some spider." David points toward the bathroom. "It's a miracle."

I make my annoyance known in small, slow movements, drop the magazine on the nightstand with a satisfying smack. "Yeah, okay. Miracle." I rise, move into the bathroom—stepping over his wet prints—and peek around the liner.

"What do you see?" The shower is running and steaming up the mirrors. A trail of water leads into the drain circled by rust and mold. The faucet's been leaking for months, a stain of orange, pink, and black splotches slowly growing above and around the drain. We've been together long enough for David to ask without asking and me to pick it up.

"Alright, I'll fix the leak when you're done."

"No! Look closer. It's something like this." David stands up straight and holds his hands out to his side, angles his face toward the ceiling. The yellow light from the bathroom makes his skin glistening and dark. He's beautiful. "Do you see anything like this?"

Squinting at the mold around the drain, I see a figure take shape, two arms curved slightly upwards, outstretched from a wispy torso, a robe maybe. A clear head but it's too big for the body, misshaped and covered in pink and black globs like a shriveled peach.

"It looks like your sister with a moustache."

David hates his sister, but his eyes dart toward the drain as if it's the tub I've insulted. "That's Jesus Christ. See, his arms are up like that. Look closer. At the face."

I'm ready with a quip, but it sticks in my throat. David's emphatic about this and I don't want to start another argument like with the salad forks. Since we've been together David's never been particularly religious. We haven't been to mass in years other than to please his dad when we're visiting Georgia. But he used to be an altar boy, was deeply devout as a teenager, even spent a semester in seminary after college.

I move further into the shower—water pelting my hair—and there He is. The brown splotches blend together in a full beard laid over enough orange and pink to create a striking skin tone. There's an effortless grin, a flush to the upturned cheeks, thin brows over amber eyes looking simultaneously up and out, piercing through my retinas but with a vision beyond. The colors are shaded perfectly, a random spool of bacteria and water laced with fluoride and rust creating an image of Jesus as clear and alive as any Christ I ever feared in Sunday School. I close my eyes and listen to water rattling on the plastic liner.

"So? You see it now?" David's hovering over me. I stand and pick his towel off the rack, dry my hair, put the towel back.

"I see the arms, but the face is a blob. Not even close to Jesus."

It's best not to hesitate when squashing bugs.

"You really don't see it?" He lifts the liner and takes another look, lets the liner fall. "It's so clear. How could you not see it?" David's hair is slicked back on his head, his shoulders moving up and down rapidly. When he gets excited he breathes with his shoulders. I'm watching his frame contract in and out, the movements of every tiny muscle.

"I'm just not making out the moldy Jesus in our shower." I smile, though I push the corners of my mouth down, pretend I'm trying to suppress it. David's upset by the remark. He turns back to stare at the drain. Steam swirls over our heads, dampens my skin. The interrupted cockroach article is fading from memory, so I ease toward the doorway. With a shrug, I'm sliding back onto the comforter and am on to the next article, exploring the latest in aboriginal medicine straight from the Mongolian flats.

For a time the bathroom is a steady sound of water tapping on the acrylic sides of the tub. Eventually the tapping is muffled and changing, David resuming his wash. He usually races through the process, but I've read my entire magazine and am well into a book chapter before I hear the handle squeak and the water cease. David emerges, dried and citrusy fresh with a towel around his waist, which I note but don't mention. I'm glancing up between every sentence as he pulls on underwear and gym shorts, covertly crosses himself in front of the mirror before crawling into bed and immediately falling asleep.

✠

The next morning I'm up before David and out jogging through the cool streets of our neighborhood. With an impending cross-country life change, I've decided in the last week to get in shape. We're in a nice apartment complex that I can run laps around, but this morning I round a few corners and enter the real suburbs, houses like a hall of mirrors, sameness down to the welcome mats. These are the Jesus people. The people who love beige carpet and acoustic guitars and feed their guilt with fake wine and beads. David and I are not these kind. We both grew up religious, felt judged, kept secrets, ran away. We both fought fiercely to eliminate our Southern drawls. Inside, we're Californians.

The sidewalks are concrete, bad for the knees, so I stick to the blacktop and dodge the occasional hatchback. I've got a nice steady rhythm going, a bounce, but I'm winded after a mile, stop frequently to walk before picking the run up again at a slower pace. When I return to the apartment, I haven't jogged nearly as far as I'd imagined. But the air will be better in California. Less humid, more oxygen dense. I'll be a marathoner in no time.

My shirt's drenched and sticks to my elbow when I try to pull it off, the slimy cloth clinging to my back. Opening the bathroom door, I'm hit by a wall of steam. David's in there, must have been for some time based on the moisture. I'm moving stealthy and hope to surprise him. The water sounds steady, the pressure hard and loud. Peeking behind the curtain, David's head isn't visible and for a second I assume he's left it running for me. But my eyes move down and see him kneeling, water streaming down his back and over his thighs to his knees, slightly cushioned by the shower pad I bought last month. If he's mumbling I can't hear it over the shower but he could be mumbling, his head down, a straight line of sight to that rusty figure I'd hoped would be gone or at least deformed by morning. The soft leaking of the faucet should have altered the image, but even from this vantage, one eye barely around the curtain, I can see the Nazarene clear as day, maybe even more defined than last night, his eyes more piercing and scowling at me over David's shoulder.

Backing out of the bathroom, I pull the door closed and lift the handle to avoid any creaking, another stalled improvement project. I open the front door and give it a little slam, stomp into the living room and build up my breathing. I hear him scrambling, knocking together plastic bottles of conditioner and exfoliant. With just the right amount of pressure I push the bathroom door open, get a good squeak out of the hinges.

David sticks his head out of the shower. "Hey. Did you have a nice run?"

"Yeah, it's a great morning for it. Clear skies, low humidity." He smiles and dives behind the curtain, the plastic snaking with his fast movement. The mirror looks like it's melting down into the sink. David must have jumped in as soon as I left, lying awake in bed as I slipped my Asics on, waiting to get back to the image.

"Didn't you shower last night before going to bed?" I run my fingers along the sheet rock, rub the moisture against my thumb. The walls are so damp the paint's coming off, the grooves in my thumbprint now the lightest shade of gold.

"I felt really hot last night, got a little sweaty. I wanted to freshen up before work." David's voice is loud and cracking. He hopes I won't notice over the sound of water splashing to the floor of the tub, but I do of course. Just like when he shrank my best pair of jeans by running them too long in the dryer and he swore he didn't do it like he was six, little tears forming in his eyes from the strain of the lie as he turned his head and tried not to look at me, just kept folding. But he knew I knew the truth and I wonder if this is the same sort of twisted interaction, David understanding that I know about the Christ in our shower and how it must fascinate him and open memories and windows he hasn't imagined for years. But does David know that I know? Would he be shattered if we had it out right now, if I told him where to shove his rusty Jesus? He's so fucking precious sometimes.

"If you felt hot, why'd you wear so many clothes? You came to bed dressed for gym class."

David drops a bottle onto the mat. "Shit. What'd you say?"

He could keep us talking in circles for a long time. I move for the door. "Just leave it running when you're done. I want to hop right in." I walk out of the bathroom and into the kitchen, wonder if our hot-water heater will hold out.

The rice in the fridge is a few days old, but after heating it in the microwave it's steaming and perfect for the garlic breakfast blend David's dad taught me the last time we were in Georgia. A year and a half in, his dad finally accepted that he and I were going to live together, so he taught me David's favorite breakfast, garlic with a dash of oil and paprika sautéed in a pan for several minutes before mixing in the rice, served with a sunnyside egg and two strips of bacon, which David and I replace with a turkey alternative. The turkey bacon's finished as I hear the water shut off. But when David walks out of the bathroom ten minutes later, the rice is no longer steaming, the white edges of his egg cold. By the time he's dressed for work and comes into the kitchen, the whole plate needs to be microwaved.

"Were you jerking off in there? I made you breakfast." I punctuate this with a kiss so he knows I'm only half serious. "See? You can still have your family's cooking when we go to Cazadero."

"God," he says before another kiss. And then after, "I'm sorry. I want to be pristine this morning. I've got a meeting with a new restaurant developer. This guy owns five upscale bars in Atlanta. Could be a big client for me." He smiles when he sits down to breakfast. I know I'm not completely lost. "Thanks. You made so much food. Eat some."

"No, I'm going to shower. I'm still gross from my run. You enjoy, baby." He gives me a look but I'm already down the hall. I don't mention that he didn't leave the water on for me. He probably notices and also decides not to bring it up. I watch him from the hallway until David's cheeks are puffy with food. His shirt is tucked in such a way that it bunches at the bottom. I make a note to fix it before he leaves.

I'm in the tub with the water on full blast. Jesus hovers over the drain and I wonder how David stayed in so long being watched in the shower by this robed figure. For a moment we lock eyes. His irises are full of detail, the shading, the movement of the lines away from the pupils. I wonder if David drew this or somehow manipulated the image into being. The water is lukewarm but then gives up and turns cold.

I rear back and spit on the rusty Jesus. My saliva's the semi-solid foam a good dehydrating jog can build on the gums. The spit hits Him on the chin where the beard is thickest and runs down the side, spreading over His outstretched hands and the folds of his robe. I hadn't noticed before the little feet with sandals sticking out of the bottom. Spitting again, this time on my hand, I press fingers to the image and rub furiously, circular motions concentrated on the face. But it doesn't budge. Figures that spit won't work, but we don't have heavy-duty cleaning supplies. David only wants natural products.

The shower creates a drumming sound, a stream smacking against my body wash, the container hollow and nearly empty. I grab it and squirt blue gel onto my fingertips, begin rubbing it on the Christ. A layer of foam covers the face but nothing comes off. The smell of the body wash fills the shower, mint and Old Spice. Rather than dissolving Him it's an anointing. I grab more bottles—shampoo, moisturizer, a bit of shaving cream—and pour some of everything into my hand, curl my fist around the concoction and mix it to gray sludge. Rubbing it in Jesus's face, I might be finally getting something off, performing an exorcism. The mixture's changing colors, flecks of rust coming apart and I'm digging with my nails now. Splashing water to clear the scene, I'm disappointed when nothing's changed. The same skin, same cheekbones, same brown eyes and little sandaled feet. I need something stronger.

David rips the curtain back, sees me huddled over the image, goop dripping from my palm. "What are you doing?"

I jump up and rub the mixture onto my scalp, hope my hair won't fall out. "Trying some new hair cream."

"Bullshit. I saw you put that stuff on the apparition. You do see it, you liar."

"What's an apparition?"

"The image of Christ you're trying to scratch off our tub." David's gripping the shower curtain so tight I think he might rip it.

"Okay, I saw it. So what? It doesn't mean anything. It's just fucking rust."

"Get out of the shower."

"I haven't even washed. I've got crap in my hair."

"I don't care. Use the sink." I know I'm losing this argument no matter what, so I do as he says, clean my hand and step out onto the bathroom mat, tilt my head into the sink and then dry myself off while David watches with his arms crossed. "I don't know why you lied. Or why you tried to destroy the miracle." That word—*miracle*—scares me, the way David relaxes when he says it. He puts a hand to his forehead, closes his eyes. "Logan, you're not allowed to use the shower."

"Like for the rest of the day?"

"Maybe longer. I don't know."

I put the towel over my head, bat my eyes and put my hands together trying to be a convincing Virgin Mary and hoping I'm matching a joke with a joke. "I shall for thee, mine son. But wherever shalt I wash thineself?"

"Shower at the gym. Use dry shampoo. You'll figure something out."

"Wait, you're serious?"

"Yes."

"So you'll keep using the shower but I can't?"

"Yes." He turns to the wall like he can't look at me. I drop the towel and the act. He's never thrown a tantrum quite like this. David's always docile, even in a fight. I'm off guard.

"Hey, it's no big deal. I'll shower somewhere else. Why does it matter so much?" I step toward him and put my hands on both his shoulders to keep them from moving. David's worked up and breathing heavy. Such little shoulders but smooth and almost completely round like tennis balls. I make it a point every day to touch his shoulders.

"I'm questioning some things. I don't know what I believe anymore. And I'm just not sure about the move, going to California. Can you just promise not to mess with the shower for a while? This is . . . I need this."

Jesus fuck Christ, I'm thinking. David's always been slightly more religious than me but he's starting to get illogical, basing major life decisions on a feeling derived from a random stain. I want to shake him, convince him to be the David I love, the one who teases me about my occasional drawl and takes afternoon walks and orders blueberry donuts from the same bakery every Saturday. I know him, but in this moment I'm struck by all that I don't know of him, this man I've been sleeping next to every night for three years. For the first time, the idea crawls around the back of my mind: *Be cautious. You could lose him.*

David's face is warm. When I wrap my arms around him I feel heat moving into my chest. "Sure. If you really need me to, I'll shower at the gym or something for a few days."

He pulls away and releases a deep breath. "Good." After a kiss on the cheek, David escorts me out of the bathroom. I want to call him baby again, but I don't.

✠

No place stings the nostrils like the grocery store cleaning aisle. Glancing at the colorful labels of white powders itches my nose as if I've been snorting the chemicals. Ajax. Bar Keeper's friend. Trisodium phosphate has a nice ring to it. I grab all three and a bottle of bleach. Painter's masks come in packs of twelve. I toss one in the cart, along with heavy yellow gloves, the kind my mother used when cleaning the tub, a box fan at full blast in the bathroom to circulate the fumes. Wearing her most hated outfit, she'd get down on hands and knees to excavate skin and dirt like an archeological dig, waving me out with chemical-stained gloves when I'd come in to pee. Loaded with products, the cart steers toward the checkout.

A human being is an unknowable thing. Cook meals together, take road trips, plan a future, feel the weight of his body in your hands, know what he can't about himself. And still he will surprise you, veer off in unexpected ways. But he's not your child. You didn't protect him from day one. What's three years of influence compared to the prior twenty-seven of his life?

If only I'd fixed that goddamn leak two weeks ago.

The powders still smell in the open air, so I throw them in the trunk of my car. Smiling the entire drive home, I feel better just having a plan. David's happy when I walk in. Salmon cakes are baking in the oven, asparagus and julienned carrots sizzling on the stove. His hair is wavy today, consequence of the humidity or lack thereof. I can never remember. His teeth are so polished. I suspect he's been using some whitening product but I haven't found the hiding place yet. We're happy strangers.

It's a quiet evening of not talking about it. I don't ask about the transfer, and David doesn't bring it up. I just repeat the town name in my head, stretching the syllables out in different ways. *Cazzzadero. Cazaderrro.* We drink wine, David showers for over an hour while I read another *National Geographic*, this one several years old and about desert elephants, their skin the texture of granite rocks. He comes to bed with his fingers wrinkled and doesn't mention the time. I get a small peck before he's snoring, clad in shorts again and this time a shirt.

I put the magazine down and watch him, one arm lying across his forehead like Scarlett O'Hara. I've never understood how he sleeps in that position but he has for three years. Only in the last nine months had he stopped wearing a shirt to bed. David's shell was thick. Religion is toxic, can cling to your skin like so much scaly rust, rebuild you in its own image. David's susceptible. Easily guilted. We need to get away to where people don't give a shit, where David can let go. He's wound so tight, can't even say no to a moldy god who squirmed out of the faucet.

David's hair is slightly damp as I pull my fingers along the top of his head, the hairs parting with ease, his breath anxious and unsteady as his eyes dart rapidly under his lids.

✠

I'm up early for a jog. David doesn't wait but rises before I've left the apartment, pretends to shower, still covering for his morning prayers. Fog has rolled in overnight, the air muggy. I can barely breathe, spend most of my time walking. A mile and a half in I scare a deer and she dashes across the street, her tail pointing to the sky as she weaves among the backyards of the suburbs. A trampoline sits directly in her path. I watch and hope to see her jump onto it, but sensibly she ducks underneath.

Back at the complex, I ease open the trunk of my car, drag out the cleaning products. David's still in the apartment—presumably washing up—but I don't want to risk being caught. The rush of the shower greets me upon entering. The supplies get shoved into the rarely used cabinet with the pasta press I bought David last year for his birthday. He used that pasta press once, never touched it again.

David walks into the kitchen, calm and happy. "Good morning."

"How was the shower?" I put my palms on his shoulders and lean in to kiss him, but he angles his face for a peck on the cheek. We're regressing. Saying goodbye used to turn into quick be-fore-work sex. Now, peck on the cheek.

"That shower is such a miracle. I feel so fulfilled." David hugs me, looks at me fully. His irises are a deep green. "God's speaking to me in a way I haven't heard in a long time. I want to talk about it tonight over dinner."

David looks like a child, like when I watch him sleeping. I may abandon the cleaning. A shower's not worth losing him. If David wants to be more religious, so what? It doesn't mean we have to be those kinds of people. He'll drop the shirt. We'll have sex again. Tonight maybe. All the time in Cazadero. We can be our real selves for once. I rub his shoulders, think about being in love.

"Yeah, let's talk about it tonight."

"Logan, I think I might need to be involved with the Church again."

"The shower told you that?"

"The Apparition, yes."

"Okay, so get involved. I'll support you." He smiles and hugs me tighter. We'll be fine. "I'm sure there are Catholic churches in

Cazadero. Plenty. We could even try a Spanish service, you know, to practicar nos español."

David's fidgeting with my shirt, picking at it like it's got a stain but it's just something to do with his hands. "Logan, I did have a long talk with my boss yesterday. I'm leaving Birmingham. But not for California."

I burrow my eyes into his. "Somewhere else?"

"I want to return to the seminary. I think God's calling me, again, to be a priest." His shoulders move up and down. He's pretending to be sad, but his face is in a resigned grin. I can feel his body, alive with energy, shaking in my hands.

"A priest?"

"It's what I've always wanted. I was too scared to do it until a few days ago, when He came to me."

"He as in the rusty Jesus?"

His smile fades to something more serious. "Through the Apparition, yes. I know this must be strange for you, and you're—"

"So you're leaving me. Let's be clear here: three years and you're leaving to be a priest?" My eyes are still trained on his, but David looks away, behind me.

"Logan, I love you. I really, really love you." He backs away, puts a hand to his chest like I'd hit him already. "But this is my calling, something I've been running from for a long time. This is what I'm supposed to do."

"Okay. I'll support you. No matter what." I'm matching David grin for grin, fidget for fidget, deep breath for deep breath.

"So, you understand?" A tear falls down the side of David's face but he quickly wipes it away.

With slow, deliberate steps I approach the kitchen cabinet, pull out the cleaning supplies. Holding the bag, I walk back to David, kiss him on the forehead. "Baby, you couldn't have made it any clearer."

I shove him hard, both hands against his small chest. David trips and lands in a chair several feet behind him. Probably for the best. I don't really want to hurt him, just aggressively work out my feelings. He's surprised for an instant, then jumps up ready to box. He'd beat me in a fight for sure, but I've already got the Ajax out, rush him and toss powder into his face. He crumbles and screams, spits and covers his eyes before groping toward the sink. I throw more powder into his hair before running into the bathroom and locking the door.

Facemasked and with yellow gloves up to my elbows, I decide to begin with what I've got open, the Ajax. I'm not doing this out of spite or revenge. David needs saving. It makes too much sense right now.

When I pull back the curtain Jesus has a bead on me, those amber irises boring into my skull. I turn my head and don't meet His eyes. The figure's still intact, and when I get on my knees and lean down I see every tiny detail, toenails and arm hair, form and muscle under the robe, the shoulders especially cut.

"Forgive me," I say softly to David. He's yelling outside the door. I dump Ajax powder on my glove and smear it over Christ's face, cover the crooked nose, the mouth, and work the gunk into his beard. The powder mixes with residual water and becomes a green, gritty paste that sticks to the side of the tub. Rubbing it in feels good, suffocating the apparition.

Wanting to be thorough, I grab the bleach with my other hand, lift it up and tip the canister over the Ajax. The mixture foams and hisses. A light gas wafts off the paste as if Jesus refuses to be undone by mere chemistry but boils with perseverance and wrath. For a moment I see the face formed in bubbles, smoke rising from the mouth and eyes. The gas is noxious and burning even through the mask. An immediate headache and I'm coughing from somewhere deep in my chest. I lose my grip on the bleach bottle and it splashes into the tub, all over my running clothes and Asics, guzzling down the drain. My nose feels like it's bleeding from the smell and my eyes can barely remain open. Through watery slits I reach for the nozzle, turn the shower on and stumble out of the tub, tripping on the edge and falling to the floor with a wet thud, still hacking through the mask. David's banging on the bathroom door and screaming my name. I crawl over to the door and lean against it, feel the vibration of his hits as I try to catch a breath of outside air. Staring back at the shower, even through tears it looks immaculate, the walls of the tub bare and clean and white as bone.

THE FEED CORN SEA

As soon as the thick oak doors of Grace Valley Baptist Church were locked, Jerry placed the half-joint between his lips and lit up. He'd had his hand in his pocket during the latter half of his sermon, spinning the crisp paper between thumb and forefinger. He'd developed a custom, taking in the smoke and letting it curl around his lungs as he walked from the back of the sanctuary to the front, where the smoke passed through his throat with a hiss that tempered the static silence. A mustardy smell filled the small chapel, covering a collection of moldy carpet, lacquered pews, and cheap wood paneling in the cloudy scent Jerry claimed was incense, something he burned throughout the week to increase spiritual concentration, keep a candle burning for God in the consecrated space of the chapel, and to keep squirrels from nesting in the rafters above the suspended ceiling tiles.

Two months and he already felt like crawling back to Kansas City, back to those downtown glass canyons that jutted out from the hills. The sidewalk anonymity of the Plaza or Westport. He'd spent the last year bartending, though he'd called it "serving tables" when speaking to the personnel committee. Gladys Mason had squirmed, but he explained how hard it was for a young preacher out there, especially one with an Old Testament Masters focused on the Minor Prophets. Nobody cared about the prophets anymore, he'd lamented. The committee had liked this remark, and he'd picked up on the subtext: love the old, hate the new. He thought about lifting his shirt sleeve to show the verse from The Book of Joel tattooed on his shoulder, but decided against it.

What the committee hadn't known was the nature of his Masters, how he'd dived into the study of Liberation Theology, Marxist thought that was antithetical to the faith-centric, infallible nature of the believers in Frisco. Jerry believed. He'd believed so deeply in college, been so profoundly affected that he'd protested, staged walk outs. Even traveled to Nicaragua, spent time in a small mountain coffee farm. But he'd earned a bad reputation. Baptists weren't interested in radicals. After graduating, Jerry had been unable to find a church-related job anywhere in Kansas City, had resigned himself to the more depressing but still ministerial role of getting people drunk.

The interview had been only a formality. Jerry grew up two blocks from the church he now smoked in, had been sitting in these coarse pews his entire life up until eighteen. Escape had been his only thought during high school. Now he'd returned, pulled back by invisible threads he thought he'd severed years before. On the phone, his Uncle Eric had talked around the issue by mentioning Aunt Rita's diabetes, David Espenson's rich son, all the tall corn. Jerry had barely been listening, switching the phone from ear to ear as he fast-walked to the bar. But his Uncle's pause made him halt.

"You know Grace Valley been without a pastor for some time now. Some of the folks around here were hoping you'd think about coming down." Uncle Eric snorted at the absurdity of the idea. "I know you like the city, but you got that seminary degree. You could do more than wait tables, Jer."

His family had always tried to bring him home, always quietly held moving away as a betrayal. Seminary had been his ticket out, a scholarship from the state denomination office. Jerry's grades were too mediocre for the good universities he wanted. He'd fallen in with the other secret leftists of the seminary, lived the life of a revolutionary. But this was over. He'd been bartending for a year, barely paying rent, with nowhere else to go. Calls were made. Interviews scheduled. And here he was, smoking in the same pew Mr. Pearson had been sleeping in not ten minutes before.

The doorknob turned and shuddered as someone tried to push. An annoyed huff, then a small figure walked around to the back of the church, the form obscured by the multi-colored glass of the windows. He licked his fingers and doused the light, pushed it deep into his pocket.

Jerry picked up bulletins, hymnals, and stray offering envelopes as Gladys Mason walked into the sanctuary through the choir loft. She held her purse in front of her with both hands. He could see the layers of foundation and powder on her face. Gladys's white hair was pulled back, gave her a youthful look until she smiled, every deep wrinkle curling on her face. "Brother Jeremiah, you sure do keep this place clean."

Jerry hated being called brother. "Thanks, Mrs. Mason. Part of the job." In small places like Frisco, pastors were also de facto janitors. Despite his disdain for having returned to his childhood church, Jerry cared deeply about the place, maintained a strict chore schedule, washed the stained glass on Saturdays. He felt conflicted every morning he walked through the oak doors, enjoying and suffocating on the familiar smells.

Mrs. Mason stepped down from the choir loft and stood in front of the altar. "Pastor, that's what I come to talk to you about. A part of the job."

Jerry wanted to put his hand back into his pocket, twist the joint between fingers, but he didn't. "Sure. How can I help?"

Her hands tightened on her purse cord. "See, we're an older crowd here, Pastor. You might consider me the youth group compared to the rest of them." She chuckled at her own joke. Nothing sounded so fake as a chuckle.

Jerry played along, smiled wider until his cheeks hurt. "Yes, ma'am. You look not a day over thirty." He felt queasy, wondered if she could smell the smoke.

"Hah! I knew there was a reason we hired you. But you see, there's some real elderly members here who can't make it to church most the time now. Stuck in their homes, you know. No kids around." She frowned and looked to the floor. Her voice moved up and down dramatically to signal what a terrible fate this was, to be without church. "Lonely folks. Some of us members were talking about how the old pastors would make visits each week to cheer up the home bound."

His stomach tightened at the idea of visiting the decaying houses of all the elderly people in the county. He saw his role as more of a teacher, not an emotional support dog. But Gladys Mason was chair of the Personnel Committee and, unofficially, his boss. This was passive-aggressive politics. Cold war.

"Sure, I could make some visits. Is there a list you could leave on my desk or—"

"I got it right here." Gladys pulled a sheet from her purse and slapped it on the altar. "Thank you so much, Brother Jeremiah. You have a blessed day now." With her last word, Gladys Mason disappeared back up into the choir loft and out the church door.

She was gone before Jerry could speak. He dropped his smile, rubbed his sore cheeks, and lifted the list. Three pages of members. Visiting everyone would take weeks. Full time. "Christ," he said then pulled the joint out, held it in his palm before placing it back in his pocket.

✠

The townspeople of Frisco called him Jogging Jerry. A few weeks ago a reporter had come out from New Helena, written a story about him titled "Racing Rev." He'd always been a distance runner, from junior high on into seminary. Running and exercise had a wholesomeness to it the elderly congregation liked, someone young and healthy in a dying world.

Frisco was set up like a square track, a few blocks of houses with two churches (Christ Redeemer, the Pentecostal cross-town rival), a school, a gas station, and a Chinese buffet in the middle. No stoplights impeded his runs, but he had to watch for tractors. The old men riding on top would wave and shake their heads, confident he'd soon give up fighting the muggy air. He could run around the town four times in an hour. Lately Jerry had been jogging early—sunrise—to avoid most of the heat and moisture. The streets were surrounded by flat farmland on an ancient floodplain. And in the depth of early August, any breeze was blocked by the corn.

Corn filled every possible space around Frisco. Some farmers planted right up to their front doors and windows. In August, the stalks were taller than any man. The corn was a force, reshaping the land, the weather, the very air. Jerry felt like he was running in a shallow canyon, wind moving just feet above his head while the humidity settled over him, his wet T-shirt clinging to his back.

Every stalk around Frisco was feed corn. Unlike the sweet, soft gold eaten from the cob with juice running down the chin, the feed corn was bland and hard as teeth. Since most of it didn't go to human consumption, Frisco's corn was loaded with chemicals. Round-Up Ready and sterilized. Feed corn was going more and more to ethanol, but the corn around Frisco got shipped to the north part of state, to the CAFO pig farms, shoveled into the fat of hogs and force-fed back to the decrepit citizens of the poverty-stricken Bootheel counties. Jerry could hardly stand running past those tall green walls knowing their place in the production chain. His Marxist hopes were as stifled as the air. The USDA called the area a food desert, but Jerry had always thought of it as an ocean. In August, the green leaves of the stalks grew thick and wide, rustling in the invisible wind like waves on a rocky shore, the sound permeating everything on unbearably hot days, drowning out the frogs and cicadas. Jerry hated the corn with everything in him.

Late at night he would climb the roof of Grace Valley, lean against the steeple, and smoke. The air was usually cooler, and the summer night brought constant wind, a small joy he forgot about during the day, its existence startling him every evening. Jerry would look out over the vast feed corn sea and think about sailors, how on long voyages they must have felt mocked by undrinkable seawater. He'd hold smoke in his lungs until he thought he might drown, then puff it out, downward, to the town. Jerry watched the stalks twist in strange patterns as if there were men darting in and among them, circling and crossing each other, their forearms bloody and cut on the sharp edges of the leaves.

✠

Jerry waited until Thursday to pick up Gladys Mason's list from the altar again. A call to three area nursing homes (the Bootheel's fastest growing businesses were nursing homes, funeral homes, and tombstones) revealed a good chunk of the listed members were dead. Jerry knew how this worked. Gladys and the committee kept old names on the list to boost membership numbers. Bragging rights were at stake, as well as money from the state association. Baptist churches were outwardly spiritual houses, but internally they ran like baseball teams: stats, numbers, and cash. These dead members would remain on the list for decades. He loved churches, loved the transformation of spirits, but Jerry hated the politics, felt drained whenever he was asked to perform some unsavory duty related to membership or fundraising or committees.

Old women dominated the list, their husbands having died ten years earlier or never coming to church at all. Jerry scanned the names, flowing past his eyes like the credits of a silent film. Opal Jean Teirrany. Verna Gallagher. Eunice Conroy. He could picture them all, confined to a chair, covered in blankets and enormous glasses, shriveled, rigid, and bitter. He wanted to embrace and run from them.

The second-to-last name caught Jerry's attention: Ruby Lincoln, his sixth-grade teacher. Though he'd grown up in Grace Valley, Jerry didn't remember seeing her in the pews. He'd known all the older ladies in the church, helped them down steps and brought them flowers on Mother's Day. He would have remembered helping Mrs. Lincoln. She had always been a school favorite, a teacher with peace-and-flowers hippie style that the principal frowned upon, though Jerry could never pinpoint why. He'd loved how Mrs. Lincoln played jazz during tests. He decided to visit Mrs. Lincoln first, save the rest for next week.

Mrs. Lincoln's house was a tiny bungalow on the other side of Frisco from the parsonage. The siding was blue and fading though it must have at one point been vibrant against the whites and browns of the neighboring houses. He walked up the cracked concrete steps and knocked. The silver top of a head came up to the window and peered through. He waved, and the door opened.

"Jeremiah Britt. You get over here and give me a hug." She embraced him with her long arms, her nails painted blue. Though slightly rounder, Mrs. Lincoln looked much like she had in middle school, her grey hair long and thick down to the middle of her back. She wore a silk blouse the same blue shade as her nails. Mrs. Lincoln led Jerry into her tiny living room, offered peppermint tea.

"Thank you, Mrs. Lincoln. Damn, is it good to see you." These were the times he didn't need a pastoral mask. Jerry felt like himself, like he did in his garden. He sat in a small red chair as she sat across from him and served the tea.

"Nice to see you again, Jeremiah. You were always one of the brightest." She reached down next to her chair into a pile of newspapers. Beneath the *St. Louis Post Dispatch* she pulled out *The New Helena Argus*, pointed to his story, to a shot of Jerry running past the front doors of the church. "I read this entire paper just for your story. Circled eight typos. You're welcome." She grinned, then lightly coughed.

"I'm flattered."

"Don't be. You deserve every ounce of praise."

"I proofread the Grace Valley bulletin, by the way. It's error-free, I swear."

She lifted her cup. "Cheers to that. I'm just surprised you're in Frisco. What brought you back?"

He wasn't sure how to answer. "The economy, I guess. I used a seminary degree to pull myself out. But it limited my job prospects so much, I had to take whatever church job I could get." He hadn't voiced it like that since he'd returned. Jerry looked out the window, at the corn. "I don't really like it here. This time of year. It feels cruel."

"You don't have to tell me that. My husband Eddie—God rest him—spent thirty years here and hated every one. Just couldn't take the landscape, flat mud mixed with these big weeds. Made him all kinds of depressed in the summer." She smiled and looked at the floor. "But you know they say folks yo-yo around here. Try to leave, you get dragged back."

"Mrs. Lincoln, do you need anything? Are there specific passages or any issues you'd like to discuss?"

"Death, if that counts. But what do you mean? What passages?"

"From the Bible."

Mrs. Lincoln sat up straighter. "I need the Bible like I need another cigarette." She coughed. "I have lung cancer. I need morphine, not vague hope."

"Your name was on a list of members for Grace Valley. I thought you'd been going and might need someone to talk to."

Mrs. Lincoln smacked her teacup onto the table, a few drops sloshing onto newspapers. "Misers. They know I wouldn't be caught dead in that place. They're saying I'm a member?"

"God, I'm sorry Mrs. Lincoln. I got a list of names and, homebound members." Jerry pulled the list from his pocket, passed it to her. He felt back in school, guilty and pierced by Mrs. Lincoln's stare.

"What's this? You got Eunice on here. She's dead. Harry, he's been gone a long time. Meredith can't even see straight. What are you playing at over there, Jeremiah? What kind of shit is that church pulling?" Mrs. Lincoln collapsed into a coughing fit, grabbed her chest and breathed deeply between each hack.

Jerry felt disgusting, looking at himself through her eyes. "I'm not trying to trick or guilt you, Mrs. Lincoln. I don't go for the rigid crap. I'm a wolf in sheep's' clothing. Or maybe a sheep in wolves' clothing. I truly want to help however I can."

Mrs. Lincoln's hand shook as she wiped her mouth with a handkerchief. "You want to help me?" She turned the handkerchief to Jerry, held it under his nose. Bloody tar, deep scarlet and black. "Get me some OxyContin. They're limiting my supply, but this shit hurts. God is the last thing on my mind." Mrs. Lincoln squeezed her eyes shut. A tear zagged between the wrinkles. "My Eddie's gone. I'm finished with the classroom. I've had a good life. I just don't want any more pain."

Jerry stood up to leave, slid the list into his pocket. "I'll help if I can, Mrs. Lincoln. I promise. I'm sorry about this. Have a good day." The door slammed behind him harder than he'd meant as he left the house. His body wanted to run, but he forced his limbs to move slow down the street. Mrs. Lincoln had twisted a screw in him, a secret fear that this place would consume him, as it had her, as it had her husband. Maybe twenty years from now he would still be at Grace Valley, fat and bald and so used to the corn it would be invisible to him, like he'd never seen a place without this green sea, like it would never end. He drifted down the flat streets of Frisco, the blacktop radiating heat all the way up to Jerry's face.

✠

In his garden, Jerry knew there was a God. Not the wispy spirit he'd been taught, not a God floating in the clouds but below, among them, in the dirt. An organic deity. He spent many afternoons cultivating this small plot of land behind the parsonage, feeling more pastoral here than anywhere else in Frisco. To his bell peppers, Jerry was a lifeline. His carrots, his sugar-snap peas, his broccoli and kale and radishes considered him a savior.

Jerry took the greatest care with his corn. He loved sweet corn plants, fragile and pale, so unlike the surrounding gritty feed corn stalks, tough as leather. The shorter, thinner stalks were like lace, susceptible to every strong breeze and rain. Jerry reinforced their roots with thick dirt from the edge of the yard. A small plot of plants, they formed a circle in the middle of the garden, a small barrier against the encroaching feed corn stalks—ten yards away at the edge of the grass—to avoid cross pollination. Jerry brushed the tassels every morning, hoped to keep his corn sugary sweet. But he also used the corn to cover the weed.

The plants were small but the buds potent. Jerry kept it on a strict watering schedule and made sure the marijuana was adequately covered among the stalks and zucchini leaves. A few weeks ago Jerry had been tending his plants when Mr. Pearson stopped by the parsonage on his morning walk, asked about the plumbing. The thin, veiny leaves had drawn Mr. Pearson's eyes immediately.

"What's that, Pastor?"

"Oregano."

Mr. Pearson had smiled up at Jerry and nodded. "Good stuff."

Jerry pinched a large helping of herb from his dry storage compartment. The dishwasher—ancient and caked with rust—rolled out from underneath the counter, leaving an empty space where he stored weed. He sprinkled the herb into a bowl filled with chocolate goo. Weed wouldn't have the same effect as OxyContin, but it was the best Jerry could manage for Mrs. Lincoln. What any real pastor would do. It had been some time since he'd mixed hash brownies, but his seminary friends had always scarfed them down ferociously, grinning like dogs.

✠

"Jonah was swallowed for fleeing his chosen path. For rejecting the plans God had for him." Jerry put his left hand in his pocket, paused for emphasis and rubbed his chin. The congregation was rapt with attention, their eyes unblinking.

"Do you run from what you know you should do? Does the Word of Almighty God scare you? All around us are whales. Things in your life that—before you know it—consume you. When we flee from the will of God, we're not looking where we're going. And we end up"—Jerry slapped his palm on the pulpit—"in the belly of something gross." He could always tell in their faces whether he had them or not. This Sunday, he did. "Throughout this next week, think about what God's calling you to do. Do you know? Can you tell your neighbor? Can you hold yourself accountable to following that path? Pray that God keeps you on his plan. His will might be painful, you may buck and fight, but it's a lot better to obey than to live inside a monster."

Usually he ended on a cheerier note, received fewer complaints that way. But sometimes it was good to twist the knife, leave them sweating in their pews. And beyond that, a little fear would get more people under the steeple next week. The Personnel Committee had been pressuring him for a greater focus on numbers. As he signaled the organ player and paced before the altar, Jerry felt as he had for the last month of Sundays: disgusted with himself. He was too good at this.

Jerry stood by the oak doors of Grace Valley and shook hands as the elderly crowd shambled single file out of the church, into their Buicks, and to the Chinese buffet. Mr. Thorton—a soybean farmer with red skin—grabbed Jerry's palm and held it. Mr. Thorton's hand was like the paw of a bear, giant and hairy with a grip like steel. But his eyes were thin, and he looked behind him to the crowd before speaking.

"That was a fine sermon, Preacher. We don't hear much Jonah around here."

"Thanks, Don. Glad to hear it resonated."

"Thing is, we don't see many whales." Mr. Thorton sniggered. "We're five hundred miles from the ocean, son. Next time, change it to catfish. There's some real monsters in the Muddy. A catfish sermon. Now, that'll preach." Mr. Thorton laughed with his mouth wide open, teeth yellow to the gums.

A few old ladies shook their heads and giggled. Jerry wanted to roll his eyes, and his pupils shook with the resistant effort. He managed to be courteous, pastoral. "Yeah, I'll do catfish next time. Just make sure you're here for it." Jerry broke into a wide smile, spoke through his teeth. "Have a blessed day."

✠

After his morning sermon, Jerry took a shower, changed into more casual clothes, and grabbed the plate of brownies, wrapped and sitting on top of the fridge. He strolled the hot streets of Frisco. Most churchgoers were napping or watching football in the early afternoon, so Jerry didn't worry about being seen or asked questions.

When he knocked on the door, Mrs. Lincoln answered almost immediately, again wearing a silk blouse and matching nails, this time bright orange. Her hair was pulled back in a tight ponytail, voice raspy and thin. "Nice to see you, Jeremiah. Did you strike my name off your membership?" She put her hand to her mouth, grunted to suppress a cough.

Jerry held up the plate as an answer. "You're off the team. I'm just here for brownies. I feel terrible about the other day. Least I could do."

"Brownies, eh? You bake these yourself?"

"I did."

"I got cholesterol numbers to watch, but what the hell. Come on inside. I'll make us some tea to go with." Mrs. Lincoln stepped aside and allowed Jerry through, then bent over in a coughing fit. He could see sweat on her forehead. Mrs. Lincoln kept a hand squeezed on her chest as she finished hacking. A handkerchief held tight over her lips muddled the sound. Jerry knew he was doing the right thing, the pastor thing, maybe the thing God had returned him to Frisco for.

"Sorry about that, Jeremiah. I guess a pastor has to get used to sick people."

"And kissing ass."

She scoffed. "You'll do well. Sit down. Let's crack into these puppies."

When the tea was done she poured two steaming cups and set them on the table. Blueberry this time. Mrs. Lincoln unwrapped the plastic, held a brownie up to her face.

"Looks moist." She took a strong bite, nodded and smiled at him as she chewed. "Well done, Jerry. How about some tunes?"

"I remember you used to play jazz for us in middle school. Do you have any Count Basie?"

"The Count of Kansas City. Good to know something I did sank in. I got a classic: *Atomic Mr. Basie*. Grab it out of the bin by the door. Record player's in the other room." She gestured with one hand, finished the brownie with the other.

It took Jerry some time to find the record, the signature red explosion of the cover. After he grabbed it he kept sifting, admiring Mrs. Lincoln's collection, admiring her. It had been awhile since he'd used a record player but he managed. The Nicaraguans had listened to nothing else. Rich sound poured out, the Count's fingers dazzling across piano keys with a fast-paced big-band sound behind him.

When Jerry re-entered the kitchen, Mrs. Lincoln was licking her fingers. He saw at least four brownies missing from the pile. Chocolate coated the corners of her mouth.

Jerry panicked for a moment. Four brownies was a lot for someone new to pot. How much had he put in? He couldn't remember. But outwardly Mrs. Lincoln seemed fine, unchanged. Her head was bobbing to the music.

"Boy, I haven't heard this in an age. Refreshing. Sit down. Take a load off."

They talked for an hour, Mrs. Lincoln about her husband, Jerry about his months in Rosa Garcia, helping locals fight barons trying to control organic coffee production. Mrs. Lincoln beamed at this story, her eyes locked on Jerry, still eating brownies.

"Hot damn. You're a real commando-preacher."

Jerry watched Mrs. Lincoln closely. He was waiting for the brownies to take effect, for her to relax and enter the same state of calm that kept him sane, that eased his own pain. Every time she lifted a new moist square to her face, Jerry tensed: *How many is it going to take?*

"So I told Vicente, our bodyguard, how hard it is to find the good mangoes in the States, but—"

Mrs. Lincoln's eyes were closed, the sunspots on her lids fully visible. Jerry edged out of his seat, put his ear to her face to see if she was still breathing. He could feel warm, shallow breath on his neck. When he pulled back Mrs. Lincoln's eyes were wide open.

"Jesus! I'm sorry. I wanted to make sure you were okay."

She laughed, quick and high-pitched, then tapped her hand on the table, her head bouncing more vigorously than before. Strands of white hair came loose from her ponytail, stuck out.

"Mrs. Lincoln? How do you feel?"

"Oh," Mrs. Lincoln moaned, and closed her eyes. Her head revolved from shoulder to shoulder. "This"—she held up a brownie—"is great shit." Her eyes flew open, met his. "We're dancing."

"Dancing?"

She looked him up and down. "Here in the kitchen." Mrs. Lincoln stood up with a speed and precision Jerry didn't think was possible after so many brownies. How many had she eaten? Eight? Nine? Rather than mellowed out, Mrs. Lincoln seemed invigorated.

She grabbed Jerry's hand and pulled him into the middle of the space. There was just enough room between the table and cluttered metal counter for them to both move around, but it was a tight fit. Jerry's sways were slight, his every effort concentrated on avoiding too much bodily contact with Mrs. Lincoln. His palms became sweaty. She let out a whoop, raised her hands and shook them. Her moves were stiff at first, small bends of the elbows and dips of the knees. But as Count Basie and the orchestra crescendoed, Mrs. Lincoln grew wild. She whooped and swung her body in circles like balancing a hula hoop. On every revolution her hips scraped Jerry's leg, but Mrs. Lincoln didn't seem to notice. Her head flipped back and forth, her ponytail totally destroyed.

Jerry shifted his weight from one foot to the other, tried to scoot away. But Mrs. Lincoln egged him on, grabbed Jerry's arm and pulled him toward her.

"Jazz, am I right? Damn." Mrs. Lincoln rubbed a hand up and down her torso. "Damn damn."

What the fuck have I done? he thought.

Jerry had always been confused when it came to women. He'd had his fair share of sex, dates, and short-term girlfriends. Bartending and the Sandinista stories were fruitful in that regard. But after moving to Frisco and Grace Valley, he'd resigned himself to his hand. Whether it was the long drought he'd been in, the warm embrace of the Holy Spirit, his own brownie consumption, or some attachment he had to Mrs. Lincoln that reached deep into his adolescence, Jerry's penis slowly became hard.

He tried to cover with unusual dancing, arching forward while bending his knees. But the effort was fruitless. As Mrs. Lincoln whisked herself around the tiny kitchen, Jerry was confident he'd fulfilled his purpose of easing Mrs. Lincoln's suffering and tried to leave. "Mrs. Lincoln, you're feeling good? You don't have any more pain?"

No one had spoken for several minutes. The sound of Jerry's voice startled Mrs. Lincoln, and she paused mid-hip shake, arched her eyebrows and looked straight at Jerry's crotch. She laughed and leapt toward him, trapping him against the countertop. A hand squeezed his biceps, and her eyes locked with his. "You know what would feel good? You know what would really take the pain away?" Mrs. Lincoln snaked a hand down Jerry's pants, brushed her fingers against his penis.

"Fucking Christ!" Jerry, pulled her hand away, tried to maneuver around her but couldn't manage without shoving Mrs. Lincoln. Her strength surprised him, her every effort bent on keeping him pinned to the corner.

"I haven't in so long. Truth is, before I go, all I want is one more good bang. And here you are." She rubbed her hand up and down the crotch of his pants, smiled at him. "Answered prayer."

Jerry shoved Mrs. Lincoln, hard like a strong chest pass. He didn't want to hurt her, knew she'd never react this way in her right mind. He blamed himself, really, for whatever the hell happened with the brownies. But the shove knocked her back more than Jerry had anticipated. Her body spun half-around like a top before she tripped and fell, her face hitting the counter with a dull thud. Mrs. Lincoln collapsed to the floor and was silent. Count Basie's piano still floated in the air.

Teeth scattered across the linoleum. A splotch of blood remained where her face had struck the counter. When he turned her over she was still alive, awake even. Jerry breathed with relief. Mrs. Lincoln blinked, a blank expression on her face revealing every wrinkle on her face. A hand went to her mouth, her fingers covered in red drool, feeling the gaps. "Eddie," she said, her voice scared and trembling. "Oh, Eddie, what have I done?"

He swallowed hard. "Fuck."

Jerry did the only thing he knew in the moment: He ran out the door as fast as his training would allow, his runner's legs slamming the asphalt with large strides. The Running Rev. From the corner of his eye, he could see church members watching him out their windows, wondering why he was sprinting at this time of day, in normal clothes. The corn stalks crashed against each other.

The front door of the parsonage slammed against the wall and cracked the sheetrock. He shut it, pulled his dishwasher out and grabbed his weed, stuffed it into an old backpack.

Jerry dashed out to the garden and began plucking vegetables as fast as he could, a thin cloud of dust rising as he darted from row to row. After the peas, squash, and bell peppers, Jerry reached for the sweet corn, tore the ears off their stalks and opened them up. He narrowed his eyes at the kernels, a deeper shade than they should have been, putrid-yellow like dark urine. He bit into one of the ears and spit out the kernels. Hard. Bland. They'd been corrupted, cross-pollinated. His sweet corn had transformed into feed. Jerry tore out all the sweet-corn plants he'd cared for, the roots fresh and covered in dirt.

From behind the parsonage, Jerry heard raised voices, people—faithful parishioners—pounding the door. He had seconds before someone would check behind the house. Every noise was obscured by the wind and thrashing corn, but Jerry discerned the low squeal of distant sirens. He threw the pack over his shoulder, turned from the parsonage, composed himself, took a deep breath, and dove at a run into the sea. His face smacked against stalks, his arms cut by the foliage. Jerry ran until the parsonage was no longer visible, consumed by a jungle of sharp leaves.

BRANSON

I'm a caring mother. My children are grateful for me, so grateful they ran off to Afghanistan. They thought I'd be mad but I just threw my head back and laughed, drove down and had a wild time in Branson. I remember my brother, how we used to conspire together under the stairs, giggle about our parents and how against them we were. Now he's fifty-two, drives a truck. Married a girl with a loose hinge and his kids hate his guts.

My children like pickles and I wonder if there are pickles in Afghanistan. If only they'd call me I could send them a fresh jar. They're pretty salty, the pickles. I'm sure they'd keep.

I read a parenting book once. It advised spanking for those defiant times so I spanked and now—Oh, Lord—what a villain I was when I told my daughter she ought to give that toddler a good swat just below the diaper line. Nothing painful, just a quick tap to let the kid know, "Hey, the world's a dangerous place. I can be dangerous, too."

How do they handle all that dust. I bet it smears their clothes, coats their eyelids and changes the color. It always looks so red on TV. I wonder if my children will come home with red eyelids.

My neighbor Beth has good kids. They all stuck around, live a half-hour's drive. One son's a deacon and a state trooper. But then their house took a heap of damage in that tornado last year, so how good could they be.

I'm seeing a counselor since my kids left. There's this thing inside me, like a new person frowning just under my skin. I'm not sure who I am. My counselor told me to talk to her—the frowner—get to know her a little. My counselor told me not to go to Branson.

My husband's name is Perry, which is not much of a name for a man. He's not a great husband. It's all wrapped up in love languages. He brings me little gifts, mostly flowers. It was nice the first time. I smiled a bit, shrugged and said "But what on earth do you *do* with these?" I told him not to but he keeps bringing me flowers. I don't know where he gets them but I'm worried they're cheap.

Perry's been so selfish since the kids left for Afghanistan. He paces the house saying, "I'm their father. I'm their father." And I sit there knitting and think "What am I, a turd?" He wants them all to himself. He was never that affectionate before they left. Now he sobs and talks about hugging my children like they're dying. The counselor called this "a reversal." I thought that sounded too fancy for what it was.

You ask anybody around town if I love my kids. I've always been loving to them, patted them on their little heads. Helped them get along. And they always loved me back. As kids they were cuddlers, burrowed their noses right up to my cheek. Now they stand across the room and stare me down with those acid eyes. Blame me for petty nothings I said years ago. It really changes your perspective on things. My counselor asked me to elaborate on that, but I didn't know what to say. He's a real fool sometimes.

My kids will be alright. They will *return* to me. They're in the midst of chaos, but God has plans for them. Ever since I bounced them on my weak knees, heard them laugh as they shut their eyes and their faces lit up I *knew* they were destined for greatness. God was going to walk through them and leave a little bit of himself behind.

Those plane people don't let you send pickles in the jar. They don't like the glass. I wonder if that's a terrorist thing. Imagine some terrorist digging out a jar of pickles, slamming it against the luggage—you'd never get that juice out—and rampaging through the cabin with the shards. Could you slit someone's throat with a broken pickle jar? My counselor wouldn't want me thinking about that.

I don't know what they're doing over there. They told me—humanitarian something or other—but I didn't write it down. I don't quite believe them, neither. They can be sneaky like that. My children. They're just too focused. They get it from me, so really I blame myself.

NEVER BEEN MORE IN LOVE

For a moment Dean suspects the unfamiliar number is no good, but he rarely receives Skype calls and he's just finished jerking off. Inhibitions are down. He's laid out on the bed, shirt wrinkled, his pants and underwear crumpled on the floor, a post-sex movie scene with only one set of clothes. This is his routine while Barbara reads downstairs. She can no longer reach the second story by herself. No real danger of being caught, but Dean feels daring for the act. Old Dean, he thinks, you've still got it.

He adjusts the laptop to keep only his face lit white against a dark room. Who would call at such a time, through such a medium? The possibilities are endless, but Dean's mind is still on the brunette from the video. And if the call could indeed be anyone, it may very well be the brunette who scrunched her face and twisted her mouth in a way that had done the trick for Dean right before his wrist became too sore to continue. Encouragingly, the call is coming from an area code unknown to Dean, which rules out a great many people in his immediate vicinity and increases the likelihood of the brunette calling. This should be a porno, Dean thinks. Women with outside area codes. He imagines her face, eyelids low and a perceptive grin that knows and had seen him. Dean clicks the green button and is instead treated to the smile of Aunt Joyce.

Dean has spent a week avoiding her. Aunt Joyce sent several emails he didn't open. She'd called and texted. Then this intentionally-off-the-record number. Some neighbor's phone, probably. A low move, he thinks, as her face pops up on the screen, her lips a bright red clashing with the heavy turquoise necklace she always wears.

"Dean! My boy, you're a sight for tired eyes. I've been trying to reach you for days."

Dean wipes his face, still a bit sweaty. It has been taking longer and longer to come, requiring more of him. He uses the wiping movement to refresh his mind, flip a smile on. Hold it together, Deansie. And for godsake, don't move the camera any lower than your chin.

From her scalp, Aunt Joyce's hair rises sharply—flatter than the edge of a cliff—before spooling out into a mass of tight gray curls. Her hair makes her look agitated like an eccentric scientist. Then there are her unnervingly intense eyes, the skin around them pulled tight in what Dean assumes was a botched surgery. She always sounds so sweet, never actually *says* anything insulting to Dean, but he is a reader of eyes and faces. She's always pestered him, has a way of complimenting his successes with an "Is that all?" tone, a lift of the brow, a pursing of the lips. His mother's sister never calls without an angle, a favor or comment to poke into Dean's otherwise low-slung and newly miserable life.

"Your screen's a touch grainy, dear. Are you still on that ancient laptop? And who Skypes in the dark? Don't you know half of age is lighting. You gotta get with the times, Dean." Aunt Joyce snaps her fingers and laughs. This is her favorite, the *despite-our-age-difference-you-are-effectively-more-decrepit-than-me* gag. It's a fat joke, really, when you strip it down. He's not a very robust thirty-nine, and she is an active sixty-four. Still, Dean wonders why Aunt Joyce can't be more like other members of her generation, wary of computers. The old bat prides herself on keeping up with technology. She holds this over Dean, sending messages and links about iPhone updates, the latest high speed capabilities, all the new pads and watches. His aunt has taken it upon herself to educate him, to pick up where Dean has, apparently, failed as a modern human being. "Step it up, old man," she says and snaps her fingers, her eternal punctuation.

Dean pretends to laugh, his lips too wide like a jack-o-lantern. He needs to match Aunt Joyce emotion for emotion, smother her in the too-muchness of his face. He smiles so hard his eyes water. "Hah ha. Yes. You're so right, Aunt Joyce, you're so right. So what's this about?"

She clutches a hand to the turquoise stones around her neck as if *he* is the one disturbing *her* evening by rudely getting down to brass tacks. "Well, I just phoned to ask," she sighs, "how is Barbara getting on?"

"Barbara's fine. Upbeat and continuing with her morning walks." This isn't true. Barbara's MS has progressed rapidly in the past three months, lesions growing like mold on nerve endings all over her body, especially afflicting her legs. Barbara hobbles around the house, hasn't passed through the front door in weeks, sleeps in a recliner near the base of the stairs, and will soon require a wheelchair.

"Wonderful. She's such a fighter. Send her my love. Stephanie sends her love, as well."

"I'll pass that along. How is cousin Stephanie?" Dean asks out of obligation but regrets the courtesy when Aunt Joyce's face brightens.

"Dean." She clutches her hands together under her chin. "I'm glad you asked."

So this is it. The favor. The duty. Aunt Joyce's purpose in calling and pretending to be interested because all her children are strung out or couch surfing well past the acceptable age, and of course they rarely talk to her but who could blame them with a mother like that.

"What'd she do now?"

"Dean! This is your cousin. Stephanie. She's not *done* anything. She's well. Quite well." Aunt Joyce adjusts a curl. "I'll have you know my Stephanie has joined the Peace Corps. She's shipping out for Africa next week."

"Where in Africa?"

"I don't know." Aunt Joyce slaps the air and huffs. Dean has apparently asked a very stupid question. "Wherever she's needed. She'll do so much good there."

Most likely dodging collectors. "Good for Stephanie."

"She just needs a little help moving her stuff into storage. I'm all the way out here in Tucson, and seeing as you're only a handful of hours from Kansas City I thought maybe you could help her, spend a few days with your cousin before she leaves for the jungle."

"She doesn't have friends in Kansas City who can help?"

Aunt Joyce frowns. "No, her friends won't do. Stephanie needs someone reliable, and you're the first name that came to mind. If that's not a compliment I don't know what is."

"Aunt Joyce—"

"I know you have your own problems. But you said so yourself, Barbara's well. Stephanie really would love to see you. And if you help her, it's like you're part of her important work in the Peace Corps. In Africa."

"I don't think I can swing it." Dean hears a faint creak downstairs, Barbara rising from her recliner. Yesterday, attempting to cross the floor alone, she broke two toes without noticing. "I need to go, Aunt Joyce."

Her red lips tighten before smiling wide again. "Well, you're just so busy. Why don't you think it over and let me know. I'll tell Stephanie you're a maybe. Don't work too hard, old man."

Dean hates being called an old man by his aunt. But it never bothers him with the guys at the insurance office or when Barbara jokes. It's said of him often. Every time someone uses the phrase, Dean gives himself an inward nod, a silent admission that it's true, has been since birth. Old Dean. He calls himself this on occasion, has always felt old, even if he's early middle-aged. The old are revered. Dean loves looking in the mirror at his gray eyes. Old people are lauded for gray eyes. In thirty years people will walk by him on the street and say, "Look at that man's eyes. Wisdom right there." And he'll think "I've had these eyes since I was a toddler. No one thought me wise then. But I was. Old Dean. Two steps ahead of the curve." But with Barbara, Dean's not sure what old means anymore.

Old people are never bothered about their weight. Dean had been a thin child. Pictures reveal an even muscular physique, a body builder in miniature. He'd maintained a slender figure until college. Then Dean met Barbara. Almost immediately his tiny gut expanded and—despite his most fervent efforts—has never contracted. But love has a way of keeping Dean from caring about his stomach. Or it used to.

Dean turns on a lamp, dresses, and hurries down the stairs, steps creaking. Barbara's hand lies flat against the wall, the other gripping her cane. Her body shakes with the strain but she has almost reached the kitchen table without Dean's help. A halfway encouraging sign. One of few.

"Why didn't you wait for me to come help you?"

She glances over her shoulder as she finally reaches the table and sits herself down, her frame hitting the upholstery with a smack. "You don't have to help me do everything, you know. I can still shake this ass sometimes."

"How are your toes?"

"It's nothing."

Dean bends down in front of her, pulls off the sock on her left foot. The two toes at the end have swollen like small sausages, red and purple and black. "Jesus, Barb. And this doesn't hurt?"

"I can't feel pain. I'm practically bulletproof. Like a superhero. There's my new career. I might as well get something out of this."

Dean's never amused when she jokes about the MS. It's not getting better. At the last exam, plaque was up almost twenty percent in a month. That number sticks in his brain. Twenty percent more neurons firing useless messages. New ones every day. He grabs a sponge and starts washing dishes.

"Please make sure you get all the little bits of egg off the spatula. It's so gross when there's crusty bits left. I'd do it myself, but I can't stand at the sink that long." Barbara's leaning on her cane, even sitting in a chair. The cane is a dark gold color, bent slightly at the top with a rubber grip that gives her right hand a permanent, burnt smell. The disease and medications have overwhelmed Barbara's body to the point of exhaustion. She looks bloated and nauseated. Her neck has ballooned, her face weary, an old beyond age that pairs with the shuffling and the arm shakes and the cane.

They had been into pizza, taken it seriously as a shared art. Dean built a brick oven in the backyard. They knew regional trends, how best to prepare Chicago style, Detroit, New York. They visited every pizza place they could, printed their own scoring cards which they'd leave on the table with the check, walk out arm-in-arm laughing at how pitiful the crust, how waxy the cheese, the idiot couple next to them who actually used the powdered parmesan. In the early years they'd taken a vacation to San Francisco for a pizza workshop, a few days spent under a supposed Italian master with gray stubble and a tall white kitchen hat which they knew was probably for show but gave the impression of money well spent. Barbara experimented with absurd toppings—smoked salmon and tarragon with a light brie—while Dean grew and roasted his own tomatoes for homemade sauces. They'd eaten every slice together, made plump by the hobby. Fifteen years of cheese and oil and dough sloshing around their middles. But Dean never cared about his or Barbara's weight. That was love. At night they made jokes about their naked bodies shining back from the bathroom mirror before curling up and falling asleep.

The strangest part about being in love—deep love that doesn't wear off, that opens your eyes in the morning, gives vivid dreams in sharp colors—was how it made Dean think about his death. They'd talked about it in bed, Dean's arms around Barbara's waist, his head resting on her breasts. "It should happen on a plane. Over an ocean."

"No." Barbara put her hand on the back of Dean's head and lightly stroked his hair. "Planes are no good. People find you days later all rotten. Or they don't find you at all."

"We'll be old. We'll both have heart attacks before impact."

"Where are we going?"

"Somewhere strange and new. Our fiftieth anniversary. Botswana. The Visayas. Siberia, maybe."

"Okay, but why a plane?"

Dean lifted his face to his wife's and kissed her chin. "So we can go quick and go together."

She was serious for a moment, her eyes wide in the dark before laughing. "Okay. Let's die on a plane together. But we sure as hell better crash on the way *back* from Botswana."

They'd been married for eight years but Dean had never been more in love with Barbara than that night.

Lately random memories have been forcing their way into Dean's mind with an intensity that scares him. Dean scrubs the spatula, works the crevices with his fingernails and holds it up for inspection.

"Bang-up job. Thank you, Honey." Barbara rocks back and forth, looks around the room. Dean knows the kitchen must appear dingy. He doesn't clean the way she likes. He's into natural products whereas she pours on bleach and every disinfectant she can find. Barbara hunches her shoulders like the room is crawling with microbes. He has to do everything—clean, cook, give her medication, help her across the room. Dean can't wrap his head around the idea that this is his life now. His mind rejects this with a ferocity and selfishness that scares him more than the memories. Sweat pools on his forehead as he's scrubbing a plate. He finds himself glancing at the back door. Why the back door, Dean? What's with the back door? It's not like you can throw it open and run away across the grass. Where would you go? Jesus, how could you consider that, even for a moment?

Dean's attention is drawn to something on the windowsill over the sink, a brown oval the size of a leaf. He brushes the curtain aside—a watermelon pattern Barbara chose to be funny—to find a large roach, shriveled and dead.

"Have you seen any roaches lately? There's a dead one by the sink."

"They come out during the day when you're gone. They're too fast for me to squash. Poor Archie."

"You've been naming roaches?"

She shrugs. "I can't read all damn day."

"How do you know this one's Archie?"

"I named them all Archie."

Dean turns back to the task at hand, the growing tower of glass and plastic and glistening metal in the sink. He pictures Barbara shuffling after roaches, their little antennae quivering as she gets near, speeding away, slowing down, circling her. They must think of his wife as an easy game for roach children. They dart and squeal and crawl up her legs where she doesn't even know they're there, are laughing about it right now under the floorboards.

"What were you doing upstairs?"

"Catching up on the news." Dean wipes his arm across his forehead.

"Who were you talking to?"

"Fucking Aunt Joyce. She said Stephanie's joining the Peace Corps and needs me to help her move her junk into storage."

"So, you're going to Kansas City?"

The dishwater disappears down the sink with a loud slurp. A long trail of rust leads in to the drain. The rust appeared sometime in the previous month. Dean can't discern any leak, but liquid must be coming from somewhere. A thought pops into Dean's head about Barbara. Maybe she's causing this, since she's home all the time now. The doctor did say she'd eventually have bladder issues. Dean imagines Barbara at the kitchen table. The urge strikes her but she doesn't have time to hobble to the toilet, so she straddles the sink somehow and realizes how much simpler this is with her condition. She starts doing it all the time, pulling her pants down and hanging over the sink, urine running down the drain and inevitably on her leg until she's so used to it she can't go anywhere else. Maybe she sneaks it while Dean's upstairs or when *he's* in the bathroom or when his back is turned. And in a few weeks—a matter of days even—she'll be incapable of even that, of shuffling to the sink and relieving herself. Barbara will wear a diaper, some oversized pillowy bit of plastic that looks more like a toy, and every day—God, several times a day!—Dean will take this off her body, smell all of Barbara's shit and piss and the way it stays there, smearing her body and penetrating the pores of her skin in a way that can never be cleaned.

"Yeah. I told her I'd go."

✠

After Barbara's asleep Dean makes a phone call to work and then one to Aunt Joyce. She answers with an "*of course* you'll help. We all know you've got to get out of there and get away sometime. Everyone has limits to what they can take and with Barbara the way she is you know you're in this fight, too, and we're all here for you, okay? It'll be like a vacation."

Dean's dreams are weird. In one he's walking through a library except all the books are orange and when he pulls one down he can't read the script. In another he's in a house that's not his house and there's a woman yelling at him from the top of the stairs. She throws a shoe and it stabs through his hand like a knife. He pulls the shoe out and ants crawl out of the hole in his palm. Dean enjoys dreaming, but he's always frustrated when he doesn't know what the dreams mean. He hates the thought that they mean nothing.

Dean wakes up early the next morning, packs a suitcase before Barbara wakes up. Folded shirts form a small pillar on his bed, far more than he knows he needs. He carries the suitcase down the stairs and sees Barbara in her chair, mouth open and one leg pinned against the wall in a way that would be uncomfortable if she could feel it. Dean glances toward the door.

"Have a good trip, honey." She uses her arms to rise up in the chair for a kiss. He puts his lips to hers and holds on, closes his eyes—if they could just stay like that—before pulling away.

"Do you need anything? Water?"

"I'm fine."

"Debra's coming by later to check on you?"

"Yes, Debra will be by."

"Okay. I'll be back the day after tomorrow."

"You will?"

Jesus, what a weird question to ask. He wonders what his wife means and what she knows, whether she could somehow hear what he packed. He'd grabbed his passport, a few family photos. All the clothes were his favorites, pieces he would have missed. She's smarter than him, which has always made Dean feel vulnerable. She has these blue eyes that grow darker, almost purple near the pupil and perfectly round like cornflowers.

"Yes. I will." He grabs the suitcase, gives a quick wave with a smile. She smiles back and takes a second too long to wave as he closes the door.

✠

The car seat is stiff with coarse fibers that itch Dean's back as he flies down a state highway, but the wheel of the car is smooth and worn in a way that feels good on his fingertips. He wonders which route to take.

What will you do when she's gone, Old Dean? Have you thought about that? How will you die then? Remember you said you'd go together. You could buy a big syringe. Take out some spinal fluid while she's sleeping. Hell, she probably can't even feel it anymore. Put it in your own neck. Can you transmit MS that way? It'd probably work. Then you'll go together. But Jesus, what a way to go. And who would take care of you? Eventually you'd both stop walking, shuffling blobs of flesh and broken bones, shitting yourselves, moaning, clawing for the fridge or the faucet until you starve or get an infection or maybe the nerves in your lungs will quit working and you can both drown surrounded by pure air.

The sex had stopped some time ago. Not only did Barbara have a hard time moving her limbs, but the act itself seemed less enjoyable to her, a celebration of a life she no longer lived. Dean didn't blame his wife, still cherished her so deeply her death would be like ripping out his own throat. But in his dreams Barbara began to change shape into something cold and foreign. His love was growing lighter. Dean has been preparing himself to leave. Through his shame, he feels a begrudging sense of pride at his own subconscious ability to survive.

Dean pulls off into a gas station. The siding of the store drips with rust, but the inside is sterile and clean. His eyes off to one side of his head, the station man is sitting very still. He's bald, a small head on a large, round body like a cherry on top of a sundae. With a giant soda and a Snickers, Dean approaches the counter. A faint voice reverberates from the back of the store, a radio preacher vehemently denouncing the nation's many unfaithful.

"Damn," the station man says, "I hate this reverend shit. But I can't stop listening to it. You tell me, dude, how does that work?"

✠

As evening draws on, Dean pulls his car up to the address Aunt Joyce gave him, a small brown bungalow in the western suburbs of Kansas City, just reaching into the less interesting Kansas side of the metro. The yard is full of twigs, the roof covered in leaves and spots of lichen and moss. But the small porch is vibrant with wind chimes, a sparkle of tinny noises greeting him as he gets out of the car and thinks about the failing synapses in his wife's brain.

"Deansie! Little Deansie!" A woman yells from beyond the screen door. She rushes out with her hands in the air. Stephanie wears fake enthusiasm like an old Halloween costume. "So glad to see you!" She's skinny, skinnier than at his last visit six years ago and with slight streaks of grey in her hair. Dean's pulling his suitcase from the backseat when she envelops him, presses herself all over in an unconscious way. God, no shame in this family. He notices the many rings on her right hand, each with a different colored jewel.

"Good to see you, Stephanie."

"Are you hungry?"

Jesus, Dean thinks, puts a hand on his bulging stomach. What a question. "I could eat."

"Cool. I know this great Italian place a few blocks away. Can you drive?"

Sure, I who drove six hours on potholed highways for the sole purpose of aiding you can now be the one to drive yet another few blocks, to hunch and squint and concentrate lest we die in a fiery crash, in which case *I* will most certainly be the one required to drag *your* limp, useless body from the wreckage. I can most certainly do this even when I see your car not fifteen feet away, a car that by all appearances is in perfect working condition and is— undoubtedly—more expensive and comfortable than mine.

"Of course. Hop in."

The restaurant is a low-lights affair that makes Dean feel awkward to be there with a woman who is not his wife. He makes eye contact with the hostess and the waiter, wishing he could tell each of them, "She's my cousin. She's my cousin."

"Thank God," Dean says as he flips over the menu. "They have pizza."

"Pizza? You're going to eat the pizza? Try the Gnocchi. Rosemary pesto on pecan-crusted duck. A salad, maybe."

"No, I have to try the pizza."

"I'm sure it's good, but pizza's just fucking pizza. Do you have the wine list?"

Two days with this woman. And does she think he didn't notice that last remark. Salad, *maybe*? She's so like her mother he nearly gags and then covers his mouth with a napkin, a cloth one in a shade of teal that strikes him as very not Italian.

"What did Mom tell you?"

"You need help storing your stuff to go to Africa."

Stephanie puts her hand on the table in shock. "Africa? She said Africa? Like it's all one thing. Mom. She's so fucking dense. I've told her twelve times I'm going to Ethiopia." Stephanie punches each syllable of the word. "E-thi-o-p-ia. I'll be working in a Fistula clinic."

"What's fistula?"

"Eat your pizza."

✠

They return to the bungalow. Dusty light from a streetlamp shines on the living room, cluttered with boxes and stray bits of clothes. A small hallway is similarly piled with not boxes—surely not boxes, of course she's not organized enough for boxes—but loose books, papers, and an array of large crystals, quartz shards jutting out in pale colors. Stephanie shows him the couch, orange and covered in knitted afghans. "Here's your little corner of home. I gotta suit up and go for a run."

"Now?"

"Yeah. I'm part of a midnight running club. I'll try not to wake you when I come in." Stephanie moves to a bedroom in the back. She emerges moments later in tight, small clothing with a plastic shimmer, a pair of running shoes in her hand. As she bends to put them on, Dean can't help but compare. She's svelte. Maybe if Barbara had been svelte—if both of them had been—it wouldn't be so hard now for her to move around or for Dean to imagine himself starting over.

"I'm glad you came, Dean. It'll be so nice to have someone else here tomorrow besides Tobias and me. Thanks for being my buffer."

Who's Tobias? And a buffer. Is that my real purpose here? Fuck it, why bother asking. "No need to thank me. It's good to get away."

"Sleep tight," she says before ducking out the door. As soon as she's gone Dean searches for the fridge.

The kitchen is more chaotic than the rest of the house. Silverware lines the counter in indistinct piles. The fridge is an older model and small. He imagines Stephanie's fridge to be filled with bottles of juice (kale goop, arugula goop), maybe wall-to-wall

Greek yogurt. But on opening the door he finds a treasure of junk: Cookie dough, chocolate milk, and a large box of Reese's Cups sensibly refrigerated. For a moment, Dean's fascinated by how little he knows his cousin.

He eats five Reese's, drinks a glass of the milk, and moves to the bathroom to brush his teeth. Dean's never given up on dental health, his favorite kind. With a meticulous ease, Dean picks bits of food from around his teeth and gums, first with his fingernails and then with a triple-thick-waxy floss, cinnamon flavored. Once finished he wipes down the mirror, takes his shirt off and observes his stomach. He places his palm just above the bellybutton and feels heat, cups the fat in his hands and lifts it like a giant sac, a new organ, something venomous inside him that could burst at any moment and lead to a world of unending embarrassment.

The afghans are surprisingly soft and keep out the draft from the living room. Dean opens his laptop, lies to himself for twenty seconds—Do you know what's happening in Europe, Old Dean? Best check the news—before he opens the folder with the brunette inside. She's balancing on the edge of a bed like an acrobat, her legs open and exposed, and as Dean begins to jerk he wishes Barbara would have tried that move. Then he forgets all about Barbara.

"Dean! Jesus Christ!"

Stephanie has burst through the door and—upon seeing Dean, fingers wrapped around his erect penis, moans coming from the screen dusting his face in blue light—sidles along the wall toward her bedroom. Unsure of the proper reaction, Dean doesn't move, doesn't hide his penis or take his hand away, does nothing to stop the brunette's grunts, growing in intensity.

"You should really . . . Just clean up after yourself," she says before disappearing into her room.

Still unsure of what to do, Dean decides the least required of him is to not finish the act. He closes the laptop and turns on his side. His body refuses sleep for some time, and not only due to his still-solid erection.

Stephanie saw his body and recoiled. Yes, Dean, you have become a hideous lump in your middle age. But was it his body that surprised her? Maybe it was the nature of the act. She probably didn't expect him to be masturbating on her couch. Some part of him should have known this was a possibility, that she could have waltzed in at any moment, sweat streaming down her neck and arms from the run. Did he want her to see? Jesus, Dean, your hippie cousin with the salads and the running club? You could drive anywhere, try for anyone and here you are laid out and exposed on your cousin's couch swinging your dick around the room. Such a charmer.

The couch springs squeak as Dean turns to face the ceiling. Just before nodding off, he realizes he never called Barbara. When he falls asleep, Dean doesn't dream.

✠

"Wake up, Dean. Coffee time." Stephanie smacks his foot with a pillow as she races by. He hears her fumbling in the kitchen. Night has barely passed. A pale light shows through a mesh of trees outside. Running at midnight and up before the sun. Jesus, this woman.

Dean rolls over and sits up with a groan. His own groggy steps toward the kitchen remind him of Barbara's attempts. He lets his feet drag, wonders what it must feel like for limbs to rebel against the body. Stephanie looks clean and fresh as if she's been awake for hours. Leaning against the kitchen counter, she blows into her steaming mug and avoids eye contact for an instant. Dean wonders if this is an apology for the egregious state of the kitchen, but he knows it is more likely a lingering awkwardness from the night before.

"We need to get ready. Tobias will be here soon."

Relief envelops him as he remembers the mysterious helper, some third person to keep them from having the I-saw-your-dick conversation. "Yeah, Tobias. Who's that?"

"My asshole ex-husband."

"I didn't know you'd been married."

She sips from her coffee. "Briefly."

✠

A few hours later Tobias pulls up in a rented truck. Dean is packing random household items into boxes, cursing Stephanie and her lack of preparedness—Who packs the day of a move? Has she never moved before? Does she know how society works?—when a tall man with short black hair strolls in. A smell of fine cigarettes wafts in with him as he smiles at Dean with faded teeth. "Hey there, fella. You must be Dean. Tobias." He extends his hand, furiously shakes Dean's. "I've heard about you. Steph's mom says you're a riot."

"Yeah, Aunt Joyce. She's a—" pain in the ass "—firecracker."

"Boy, you got that right." Tobias laughs, high and squealing like a porpoise. It's annoying and endearing at the same time. Dean can't picture him any other way. Tobias is a human dolphin, playful and harmless. Dean resists the urge to pat him on the head.

"Toby! Come look through any of this shit you want," Stephanie yells from the back of the house.

Tobias looks down the hall and sighs. "Alright, buddy." He slaps Dean on the arm. "Here we go."

Stephanie assigns Dean to the living room, which has all the biggest furniture and—of course—all the crystals. "They're full of calming energy," Stephanie says. "Please be careful with them."

Careful. If he dropped one on his foot, it's his foot that would need care. The crystal would be fine. They're an odd pile of rubble, two dozen or so formations in varying shapes and weights, from the size of an apple to that of a small chair. Each is much heavier and more awkward to carry than Dean anticipates. They are, at least, mesmerizing, a swirling mineral formation inside the rocks being the chief feature, what Dean assumes is the "energy." Stephanie and Tobias argue throughout the bungalow as

Dean waddles rocks to the back of the truck. The crystals are jagged with large pointed quartz structures. He imagines tripping on the steps and landing on a crystal, his neck or face hurtling downward, resulting in some kind of grotesque injury, something difficult to explain back home.

"Dean, was it you got that dent in your head from Iraq or Afghanistan?"

"Neither, sir. Crystals. Ones full of calming energy."

Once he'd moved the crystals Dean started in on the furniture. A large cabinet sat against the far wall. Dark wood and intricate carvings. Must have come from Aunt Joyce. Dean lifts one side but it's too heavy. He opens the drawers and finds them brimming with batteries, postcards, candles, tax papers. My God, Dean thinks. She's like a child. Who doesn't take the shit out of the drawers? My idiot cousin. No packing sense. There are dust bunnies blowing around this living room like tumbleweeds. Is she going to clean? Is she going to do anything? Will I—Old Dean— be stuck here moving worthless papers for days? A week? Maybe there are other rooms I don't know about. Other floors. The bungalow goes down twelve stories. Ten of those stories are crystals, all orange and pink and spiked like a mace but still filled with that calming energy. Calming, calm. Oh, so calm.

I wonder what my wife is doing. I wonder if she thinks about me. Maybe she can walk again. Maybe she's better and dancing in the kitchen with Archie the cockroach and is waiting for me to burst through the door and hug her and hold her up and say, "I knew you were in there. I knew you were hidden in that woman. I knew this wasn't real life."

Stephanie strides out to the living room just as Dean—having removed the drawers—tries to pick up the cabinet. "You'll never get that by yourself, you idiot."

Yes, he thinks. *I'm* the idiot here.

Stephanie lifts the other side, wheels around and starts to back out the door. They're taking it slow. Dean strains, finds he's holding his breath for some reason.

"Marriage is so fucking awful." She stops moving and looks pensive, thinks to herself as she—and Dean—hold the cabinet. Dean's arms shake, his teeth grit.

"Uh huh."

"Tobias was like a parasite, needed me for everything. He actually wanted us to do all the chores together. Like we're going to bond over dusting and pulling weeds and shit."

"Yeah."

"He's so helpless. Marriage is for needy people. Everyone knows that. I mean, come on, you're a good guy and all, but I can see it in your face, Dean. You know." Stephanie moves to the truck. They slide the cabinet toward the back and secure it with boxes.

Aren't all people needy people, Dean thinks? Does Stephanie imagine herself as without needs, some hermit who can run off to a remote hill in Ethiopia and live this noble life with her books and her crystals, helping solve the fistulas and feeling superior, so goddamn unearthly superior over them, the needy couples of the world? He looks over and can't stand the sight of her, imagines how ugly she must look—how ugly everyone looks—when they're naked, moving a cabinet or a chair. Dean's at least grateful she hasn't worn her tight running outfit.

Tobias walks out, wipes his forehead. "You and me, bud, let's start on the kitchen. We'll grab the table, and from there it's just a shitload of boxes." He laughs. Dean can't see what's funny.

✠

An orange glow fringes the horizon by the time the house is emptied and the truck loaded. Tobias drives off with a wave and a wink. "See you tomorrow, bud. Then we have fun with the unload."

Dean's forearms are drenched with sweat. His body feels sticky and sore. So it's a surprise when he walks back inside the bungalow and realizes his couch is packed away. No concession has been made for his comforts. Great, he thinks. It's the floor for Old Dean. I who carried the rocks and the boxes of cast-iron pots and the antique oak furniture will now sleep on the floor like an animal, like Stephanie's trained pet. Maybe I'll get lucky and she'll feed me. Perhaps she'll let me out later to shit in the yard. We can wave to the neighbors while I'm on a leash with my pants down and my tongue out with drool sliming down my chin.

"Dean." Stephanie stands in the hallway. "Come back here." She walks to the bedroom. He hasn't seen it. Stephanie and Tobias moved all the junk in her room but there must be something else, some cabinet she hopes he'll walk to a dumpster she knows about three blocks away.

He expects the room to look like an antique store but is surprised to find it clean. No piles of books or weird statues or incense burners. The room is simple in bright colors and—goddammit—full of calming energy. Stephanie sits on the bed.

Dean rubs his chin. "You didn't pack the mattress."

"Not yet." She sits up straight, which outlines how tall and slender she is. Stephanie takes on a business tone. "Dean, I'm going away for a long time. Two and a half years, at least. And you—" she pauses "—you've got Barbara to deal with. I imagine—considering last night—you're not having much sex. So, I'm proposing that we have sex. Together. Here." She folds her hands, leans in. "What do you say?"

Thirty seconds ago Dean would have found the idea repulsive, but now desire condenses within him like a storm. A high-pitched static fills Dean's ears, the firing connections of his own electrically charged neurons deciding what to do. His penis is already responding to the sense of being wanted, a thing he didn't know he'd been missing until this moment. He wills himself to think about Barbara, but his mouth turns dry and Dean faces the hard fact that even this will not stop him. Even the idea of his wife staggering to a table or chair or the bathroom or trying to climb the stairs, and then the image of her falling, her face striking the floor and jiggling with impact, roaches crawling around her, her unable to call someone and being nothing more than thirsty. His mouth is dry not with guilt or embarrassment but with a penetrating need that stares his wife in the face and hopes that she'll die soon, that a merciful God will shoot them both.

"Okay."

They begin slow, fumbling with sweaty clothes, dodging each other's mouths until the connection is made and it lasts. His hands are shy and then he takes over, some funnel of emotion Dean's never felt before driving him forward. Dean feels stripped away from his layers of skin, every suppressed thought let loose. He grows rough with Stephanie's body, lifts her up and draws his coarse tongue along her stomach, makes what he thinks are masculine noises. She moans but it's not like the brunette and he wants it to be just like that. The sex is tumbling and rough and jagged, Stephanie beneath him then on top then beneath him again.

When it's over Stephanie lies back on the bed and stares at the ceiling panels for a long time. "Oh my God. Dean. That was great," she says with surprise.

"Yeah." Curling up on one side of the bed, Dean thinks about planes, about the proposed trip to Botswana. Stephanie felt like that. He anticipated a crash or a heart attack. Something you're not supposed to survive.

Maybe Barbara really has collapsed on the stairs. Maybe she's writhing in agony and waiting for him to help her up, her lips parched and calling his name.

Grabbing his pants from the edge of the bed, Dean dresses in a fury. His hands shake on the zipper, seized with a desperation to touch his wife, smell her pillow, hear her drawing breath.

"Where are you going?"

"I don't know. Just going."

"There's always a kick to this."

"A kick to what?" His shirt feels clammy and damp but he throws it over his head anyway.

"Cheating. You get this emotional backlash. Part of the experience." Stephanie puts her hands behind her head. "Ride it out and it'll pass. I mean, this is good for both of us."

His shoes squeak against the floor as Dean forces them on his feet. How could you have literally slept with the enemy, Old Dean? Think of a comeback, any kind of comeback. "You're just like your mother." Dean stands up, faces Stephanie and sees her smug face unchanged, as if she didn't hear him. Yeah, that was brilliant, Dean. You're just like your mother. And I just fucked her. So I've just fucked Aunt Joyce. Now look how low you've sunk, you slug. He walks out of the bungalow, throws his suitcase in the car, and drives off.

✠

Dean winds into the heart of Kansas City and circles the bowl of downtown interstates looped around skyscrapers. His brain knows which way is Barbara, but some part of him resists, feels the urge to keep running. You're already this far. Why go back? Why make it harder later, when she gets worse and can't speak or sing or laugh or use the toilet or the shower or be anything at all? Why watch that happen to her?

He drives the loop for an hour, winding past the same exits and row houses and shimmering windows. But the image of Barbara waiting on the floor, alone and in need, compels him to turn the wheel toward home. The sky grows dark and he passes what seems like an endless field of corn and soybeans and streams, the occasional gas station as an oasis. He doesn't listen to music, doesn't think. Dean decides to quit arguing with himself, ties that base person—the inner Dean—to a chair and gags him until he's at his own front door, key in the lock with a soft click.

Her chest rises and falls. She's asleep, healthy and safe. Barbara. He watches her for a minute before he can't help himself, touches her arm, buries his nose in her hair and kisses her.

"You're back already."

"I am."

"Why so late?"

"Let's get on a plane. We can go anywhere you want. We'll fly around the whole world until either our money's gone or we crash. I'll even make the plane crash. I'll do that for you. Let's go, Barb, let's leave right now."

She grabs his hand, brings it to her mouth and kisses it. "I missed you. Thank you for coming home."

He doesn't have to wonder why she thanks him. Only how he's going to live his life without her.

✠

Months later, Dean gets a Skype call from Aunt Joyce. Her hair is the same fluffy gray, now accented by pink lipstick that works slightly better with the turquoise necklace. "Dean, my boy! How are you holding on? How's your lovely wife?"

"She's fine, Aunt Joyce. What do you want?"

Her hand clutches to her chest. Of course the hand goes to the chest. What else could the woman possibly do? "Well, I just *want* to let you know how Stephanie's getting on. Especially since you left her high and dry with her move half done. She's been doing wonderful work in Africa. The women over there just adore her. Very successful, my Stephanie. She's—"

"Hey how about that, Aunt Joyce. Gotta go." The laptop snaps shut.

Dean walks down the stairs, seats himself next to Barbara's wheelchair. One eye follows him, the other falling off to the side as her mouth opens and closes. Dean hears soft clicks from her throat but she can't put the words together. She stopped being able to read or speak weeks ago.

Dean wipes saliva from Barbara's jaw then wraps his arms around her. He pictures all those sparkling neurons within her sending signals to nowhere. Dean puts his ear to his wife's head and hears a light buzzing, the electrical messages trying desperately to get across. With his brain inches from hers, he imagines the scarred tissues might strike lightning across the chasm of cells between them, reach into his skull and transmit one clear thought: "I'm sorry. I love you. You can leave me."

He pulls away and looks at all the features of her face, every special bump and wrinkle he'll remember forever. But Barbara doesn't look back, her eyes drifting off to some foreign country far behind him.

GHOSTS ON TV

In 1937 my father walked into my bedroom, looped a rope around my neck, and pulled. The rope was for the horses, coarse with little fibers that stung my skin. I was eight years old. Dad was so desperate, using all his strength as if he were being crushed under some giant weight. He'd just caught Mom with another man, strangled them too, but not before Mom confessed I wasn't really his daughter. After he killed all of us in the house he shot himself through the chest. Of course I didn't know that at the time, had to skim it later from all the police moving through.

I don't recall a moment of waking up into this. I was alive and then suddenly I wasn't without a clue what to do next. After the police were gone I laid myself out on the floor in my room, and I think it was years until I got up and left the spot where they found me.

Now I'm with Cynthia. She's just lost her husband to another woman and the loneliness seeping out the doors and windows smelled irresistible. It wasn't Cynthia's house that I died in but I was just down the street, close enough to move in.

Loneliness smells like fresh apples. Earthy and cold. It was tasty at first but it gets old eating the same thing all the time. Sometimes the loneliness repulses me. Other days I'd peel off someone's skin just to get a drop. But I'm not that desperate anymore. Cynthia produces it like a fog machine, the loneliness melting right off. I follow her wherever she goes in the house. Walking down the stairs. Dusting shelves in the living room. Making sandwiches at the counter. Sometimes she forgets, still makes two.

I don't understand why I'm here. I know all about unfinished business, but I got over that a long time ago. Was it something I did? Was I a bad kid? Do I need to fix someone else's life the way my dad thought he was fixing mine? You'd think that'd be his job. But he's not here. I've seen others wandering around, but never my family. It bothers me that they all died at peace except me.

When I finally left my old house I approached a few others like me, asked what this was about. They gathered around in a circle, smelled me up and down. Then they walked on without a word. They're no help. Out here we're all on our own, try to avoid each other. We're unpleasant when we're hungry.

Cynthia has a cat named Sheba. Sheba and I hate each other. While Cynthia's gone all day I usually step on Sheba's tail. She'll turn and hiss, but she can't see me. She just feels it. Sheba's all alone but she's not lonely. Doesn't give off a whiff.

The first thing Cynthia does when she comes home is cry. She puts her coat on the rack, looks out the front window, then moves toward the stairs. It's always the stairs, like the space triggers her tear ducts. Maybe it's where she was when he finally left. David. He's very handsome. I know because his pictures still line the halls. After crying Cynthia will walk by the pictures, touch every one. Then she watches TV.

I remember the moment I woke up to Dad strangling me, the lines around his eyes etched clear and deep by the light from the hall. He had black and white stubble, his lips back with his teeth grit. Like he hated me. But I was a good girl, listened to every word he said. In those last moments I thought it was me, that I deserved this somehow. It never occurred to me that he would be the one who was wrong.

Stupid. I know that now. I hope that wasn't the reason I'm here. I just wish I knew what to do. There's no manual to this.

I'm fascinated by the TV. I always watch whenever Cynthia's watching. I never had anything like this growing up. These strange, fluid stories, these actors moving in their pre-set rhythms from weeks or years or decades ago. Sometimes I imagine they're just like me, stuck and starving.

I've been with several families before. It took me ages to figure out how to eat. Once I had enough loneliness I could start to move things, create smells and feelings. Cold air. My dad used to catch animals in the woods, set up traps for rabbits or little squirrels. It's like that, laying things down so that you could squeeze out enough lonely to have a satisfying meal. It doesn't take much, just the slightest prompting to make people lonely. You do feel a bit bad, encouraging this negativity. Which is why most of us don't stick around one place for long. You can be hungry and still feel guilty about it.

I'm taking my time with Cynthia. She gives off so much loneliness without any prompting, though I can smell there's more in there. But there's no rush. And in the mean time I enjoy the TV. Cynthia likes cop shows, especially dark ones. The crimes are gruesome, the bad guys menacing and vile, their victims traumatized or scarred or angry or dead. Sometimes the cops catch the bad guys, sometimes they don't. You'd think this would upset her, but as Cynthia watches she feels better. Her loneliness dissipates and the air in the room is completely clear. I think about using my energy to change the channel, but it's nice to see her happy sometimes. And she'd probably just change it back.

Cynthia always makes small noises or groans or little twitches with her eyebrow or mouth while she's watching TV. I spend half my time watching her rather than the screen. I wish she'd say something. Let me know what she thinks. I wish I could peel back her skull and get a look at what's going on in her brain. You'd think a thing like me might have that power, to see through people into who they are, what they know, how they want to be. But we don't. I don't think anyone anywhere has that power.

My dad took us to a county fair when I was five. That was the first and only time I ate ice cream. French Vanilla. I had on a blue church dress and a little straw hat. The cone was so large Dad had to hold it for me while I licked. The ice cream melted and ran everywhere, ruined my dress. Now people eat ice cream all the time. Cynthia has some every damn day. I wish I could taste it, wonder if it's the same as I remember. Sometimes I try to lick Cynthia's ice cream but for me it's just dirt.

I wonder how much influence a single life could have had on the world. What would have changed if I had lived? Could I have stopped WWII? Would I have invented a miracle vaccine or saved a species from extinction? Maybe the opposite was going to happen. Maybe I would have become a serial killer like my dad. Maybe I'm here paying for all the bad things I never got to do. More likely, though, the world would have been largely the same. I believe that sometimes, but if the world didn't give a shit about me why am I here? I have to mean something to still be around.

While he squeezed the life out of me my dad didn't say a word. His face barely moved, like it was a mask. But I could be misremembering. You'd think without a physical brain to be faulty your memories would clear up, but it's not like that. It's more of the same fogginess.

One night the cop shows are all reruns. Cynthia flips around until she lands on a show about ghosts. There's this woman in a room, spotlights on her and tears rolling down her cheeks. She's talking about her childhood, the haunted house she grew up in. Then they've got these stiff actors doing everything she says, really hamming it up. Screaming and crying and throwing plates. For a moment I worry Cynthia might get ideas about me, but she just scoops more ice cream.

In this show the ghosts are assholes. I mean they're really going after these people. I can't say I wouldn't do the same if I was starving, but these people seem plenty miserable, like they should be giving off loads of lonely. Or at least the re-enactors make it appear that way. Is this what I should be doing? Should I be scaring the shit out of Cynthia on a daily basis? Whisper into her ear at night that she should break a mirror or skin the cat or scratch "YOU DIE NOW" on the wall?

This TV is really something, how it squirms into your brain.

I'm absolutely gorged on Cynthia's lonely. I'm so stuffed I have time to worry about her. You'd think a person this lonely would talk to themselves nonstop, but Cynthia hardly says a word, to the TV or the cat. Not even when she looks at David's pictures, brushes them with her fingertips and pulls on her hair.

I wonder what my dad was thinking. Was he so embarrassed he needed me dead? Did he forget the time he bought me ice cream? Or when he taught me how not to be scared around horses? You can ask yourself a million questions about what happened and no matter how many times you ask the answers never appear. Only questions echo back.

Apparently there's such a thing as giving off too much lonely. The other day another one like me came sniffing around. Popped right through the front door while I was on the stairs. He licks his lips, tells me he knows about all the good grub in here and to quit playing with my food. I respond by ripping his fucking head off. No one's haunting this house but me. And Sheba.

I decide to try it, harass Cynthia just like the ghosts on TV. I'm satisfied enough, but I wonder if this is part of my purpose here, if going after her will help me move on. It's boring, this slow floating life. I'm anxious for something else.

I spend a few days building up loneliness until I have enough energy for a spectacle. While Cynthia's parked in front of the TV I make my way upstairs. Sheba's on to me and follows, but I don't mind. I wait a few minutes and then slam the bedroom door. Cynthia runs up the stairs, takes them two at a time. Like she's rescuing a person. I wonder if she's forgotten again that David's gone. Or maybe she thinks he's come back.

When she opens the door to see no one but the cat, the lonely pours from her in clouds so thick I can't see across the room. It's a heavy meal, but I'm curious about what happens if I push it. Cynthia's still, her hand on the knob. Then she turns to go back, leaving the door ajar. I wait until she's down the hallway—her foot hovering over that first step on the stairs—before I slam the door again, harder than the first time. She leaps, nearly trips, puts a hand on her chest and watches the door. When I've got her full attention, I turn the knob slow so she can see the movement, open the door with a long squeak. I see it building in her face, raw fear. We're two actors hamming it up. Just like TV.

I spend so much time thinking about my dad, I've almost forgotten Mom. The memories are unclear, but I know she was pretty, and not just in that way that all little girls think their moms are pretty. She was Miss-Teen-USA beautiful. She wasn't around as much as other moms. Whenever I picture her it's always from a distance, Mom high in a saddle. She rode every day, sometimes for hours, she and the horse strutting off and over the horizon. She must have been lonely, maybe had someone like me tracking her out there. I wonder if she thought about me like a real daughter.

Cynthia flees downstairs but after an hour she comes back and gets ready for bed. As she lays herself down I'm there beside her, where David would have been. I think I might enjoy this new phase, the real haunted house stuff. I don't recognize myself, how cruel I can be, how much I'm looking forward to driving her crazy.

Cynthia's almost asleep when she reaches a hand over, rubs the sheets. It's rare for our bodies to cross, but it's happening now, her hand at my shoulder blade. I know she can't feel me, but her touch is so warm. Cynthia leaves her palm there, her eyes closed and her whole body so still. "Not yet." She says it lightly, turns over to face the wall. I move my fingers through her hair, and for just a moment I let myself believe this is all about me.

IN THE CLOUDS

Although he'd spent all morning gazing at their slick, dark bodies dotting the sky, the purple martins were a diversion. If the neighbors were to peek out from their curtains, they would perceive only a crumpled old man birdwatching. Elwood could sense their eyes on occasion, some passing glance as they crept down a hallway or closed a bathroom door. These new neighbors—young couple with no children—had become a nuisance, hosting other irresponsible, childless couples at all hours of the evening. They never went to church, as far as Elwood could tell. Rose thought she—the wife—seemed sweet, but Elwood didn't care for these people, some suspicious new color in his world. Undoubtedly, the couple felt the same about him. He was palpably aware of being underestimated, an annoying social sense he had acquired in his golden years.

Later that afternoon, his grandson Jacob came and sat in the lawn chair next to Elwood. Young and cocky, smiley for no reason: Jacob wore the same stupid grin as nearly everyone in Elwood's life now. He could never understand what everyone was so happy about. They chatted for a bit, Jacob going on with some asinine story about how his daughter Emma lost her first tooth by a fly kickball. Elwood listened as patiently as one could at his age, on this day.

"We get this call from the school, and she's always been a good kid, so you know it's something bad. Claire just flips out. She wants to go get Emma, but the nurse says she's fine."

"Suffer the little children to come to me," Elwood's tenacity would not allow this final opportunity to pass.

"What was that, Grandpa?"

"For only he who seeth and liveth as the child will enter the kingdom of heaven. Thus says the Lord. It's in the Book." Elwood put on his staunchest frown, every wrinkle pronounced as he attempted to convey urgency. There wasn't much time.

"It sure is, Granddad. So, when we got that call from the school we thought Emma'd come running home crying. But my tough little girl walked off that bus smiling with this great gap in her teeth, holding that lost tooth up in a little bag." Jacob pulled his lean frame up in the rusted lawn chair, his clean face radiating as small crow's feet curled around his eyes. "She's just as proud as she could be."

"You ain't teaching a girl right that way. Let not your heart fill with the selfish ambition or vain conceit, fleshly things. The Lord says that, too."

"Yeah, I know he does. So, Emma, she—"

"Jacob, boy," Elwood leaned over, placed his hand on his grandson's thin shoulder, "you ain't hearing me. He's coming today."

"Who's coming, Grandpa?"

Elwood's eyes grew sharp, poised to transfix his grandson. "The Lord. In the clouds. Coming to gather his host." Elwood's grip tightened on his grandson's shoulder. "It's the day of the blood and the tribulation, so you, Claire, and Emma all best go. Pray and prepare. To meet him." He spoke in a low and reverent tone, a gospel cadence of plunges and crests.

Jacob sighed, shifting in his lawn chair, not—as Elwood had hoped—out of conviction, but as a non-verbal cue that he wasn't taking this guidance to heart and would soon leave. "Granddad, why would it be today?"

"Jesus come to me this morning, whispered it to me, in my dreams. I've seen it all laid out. Sure as the sunrise, this is the day of the Lord's vengeance."

Jacob sat back, closed his eyes, and smiled. Elwood saw the shakes of his suppressed laughter. "Well, you keep a lookout for me. I'm gonna run on home and take Emma to the park."

"There ain't no running. We all gonna be found in the full light of God when those trumpets call. You be smart and be ready. It's the end we've been promised, coming soon."

"Just keep a watch for us. I'm gonna go inside and check on Grandma." Jacob stood, cleared his throat, gave his grandpa a slight nod, and sauntered off. The air grew soft and quiet as the purple martins hid from the heat of the day.

✠

As the sun sank behind the neighbor's roof, purple martins re-emerged to storm the dusky sky. Their bodies tumbled and cork-screwed to capture the evening's mosquitoes. Elwood couldn't wait to have wings, to duck and plunge whenever he wished. He felt small, even compared to the birds, but he sensed the approaching hour and knew he had only to wait.

He remained vigilant, but Elwood was seething over the patronizing attitude of his grandson. If Elwood was honest with himself, he'd already known Jacob would not accept the Word, though he'd felt compelled to try. Even if he never understood his grandson, Elwood wanted to connect. But these young people were so far gone. If only he and Rose had raised Jacob's mother Catherine right, instilled respect for the heavenly things. Jacob was too much a part of the world. Like those wine-guzzling neighbors, always lounging on the patio with those same, lazy grins all young people had now. Jacob couldn't see beyond tomorrow. But really, what does a boy know of time and visions?

Elwood had become creaky and sluggish in his waking life, tired of the small, lusterless chores of the everyday. Food had ceased to taste as vibrantly as it had before, his legs barely had the strength to mow the lawn, and his own speckled skin felt like a grey, cracked substitute. Worse still, his wife had become a useless social cause, a parlor-room parrot who couldn't hold more than one thought at a time. His whole life had worn and frayed its once sharp edges.

But at night, Elwood lived a full-bodied life, deep and strong, tasting of sweet, dark syrup. Memories of his entire existence could be sequenced, revised, and relived a hundred times in a single night. Catherine was a sweet little girl, splashing in the tub as Elwood dipped a cup, titled her head, and poured over her. Rose was lively, baking rhubarb pies and making jam from their persimmon trees. Over and over, the same dresses and skinned knees and walks to church and barbecues and sacred confidence in the projected paths. Once collected, all these details and moments distilled to some potent, heightened truth. Just before the product of every revelation and prophecy would lay bare for Elwood to fully perceive, the vision would dissolve as he slowly, sorely woke up.

Last night he'd slept deep, ran through all the memories many, many times. But this night, at the end of his dreams, Elwood lingered, witnessed the Holy of Holies, felt a clear whisper. He'd sat up quickly. Elwood felt more confidence than he'd had in years, knowing the memories led somewhere real and proven to him. He was blessed with the knowledge of the Lord's Day.

Through the twilight, Elwood saw Rose slide the heavy glass door and waddle toward him, yellow rubber gloves covering her hands. Her steps were unsteady, and her chin shook slightly. Plump and unaware, she leaned on the empty chair next to him, peering up at the few emerging stars.

"You should sit and prepare yourself, Mother, for he cometh soon, his mouth a sword against those who ain't ready. We should watch the clouds."

The martins had just found their nests for the evening. Soap suds crinkled along Rose's forearm as she held up a saucepan, some charred dinner in the bottom. "I've just made you and the kids some supper, Father. You should come and eat. Tell little Cat not to swing too high."

Elwood sighed, lightly patted her hand. "Catherine's long gone, Mother. There's no use in eating or sleeping. Like a thief in the night it shall be, and I'm gonna be watching."

Rose squinted and bit her lower lip. She winced for a second, then, exasperated, let out a long breath. "Well you have fun at the game." As the sky fell completely dark, Rose turned and cautiously made her way back to the house. She struggled with the glass door, waddled back inside.

Elwood wasn't concerned for his wife, feeble and weak-minded as she was. She'd be taken with ease, like the children of the world, spared. The others, his grandson, Elwood didn't understand. He'd arranged his life to the book, as it foretold, and now the world and its people were beyond knowledge, possibly beyond saving. Common sense had forsaken the age.

But in those dreams. Eating biscuits at his mother's table, running his fingers against the harsh grain of the wood. Pulling sticky lumps of white cotton as beetles crawled out the stalks. The lacquered wood and crimson drapes of the tabernacle, how his knees had made dents in that floor, his tears darkened that carpet. Sweat dripping into the edges of his eyes as he worked one end of a saw, back at the mill. Burying his father. Wrestling his brother. Rocking to sleep his only daughter. These were the recursive fruits of life, and Elwood gorged every night, disappointed every morning, lacking faith in the day. Elwood had been waiting to die, for the end of dreams, a life awake.

A gentle breeze whisked his white hair. Elwood had resolved not to move until it came. His chin bobbed with fatigue. He could feel his dreams approaching, melting into the real world. The occasional bat flickered against the light of the house. His neighbors' porch was a pale shadow against the dark sky shimmering with infinite crystal light, a single cloud obscuring the moon.

A CROSS IS ALSO A SWORD

Reverend Billy Gadsen filled both containers to the brim with gasoline. Ten gallons would be enough. His arthritic fingers spun the cap of both cans until they gave a satisfying plastic snap. His right hand was sore from the effort, and he cradled it awhile before standing up and lifting the red drums into the back of his truck. Sniffing the acrid but pleasing odor on his fingers, he plucked a comb from his back pocket, fixed his thin, white hair before climbing into his truck and pulling out of the station.

Billy drove slow through the small town of Limburg. The sun was just rising, every tree and mailbox and telephone pole a palette of cool blues tinged with red on the edges, the red giving the impression of spears or dripping blood. Working in ministry, Billy saw blood everywhere. Pastors should be comfortable with blood. But he'd never had that gift, had always been sickened by those gory crucifixes. He made a few turns and ended up on Main Street. Billy stuck his head out the cab window, a faint breeze curling around his face and twisting his hair in all sorts of directions. In the rearview mirror he saw liquid jostling through the translucent plastic of the cans. But both stayed upright and in place.

Houses rolled by, people and families Billy had known from their births. The Quinns were rising to the chime of their antique German grandfather clock. The lights of Terrance McDowell's bedroom were dark. Probably sleeping off his graveyard shift at the shipping center. Terrance's neighbors—Jamie and Tiffany Bradford—owned a used car lot close to the interstate. Their white-sided house cast a shadow over a rusted playset, the

Bradford kids Michelle and Darren now too old for the thing. This was Billy's territory, his people, his flock. He watched over them as they slept.

He'd never cared for the shepherd metaphors, thought of himself as more of a Roman centurion, a stern soldier in gold, purple, and crimson Biblical regalia, the outfit men of the church wore during Easter pageants. Those same men who cried at prayer service, who smiled and shook hands in Sunday School, would put on those uniforms and transform into brutal warriors tossing Jesus around the stage, bringing down the plastic whip (the sound effect always off), hammering retractable nails on his palm. The men took joy in the performance, in the acceptable release of violence. As the reverend he was spared that duty, instead appearing at the end of the play in a sweater vest to guide any lost souls in prayer. But sometimes he'd sneak into the storage room above the baptistery, pull out the old costumes and wear them around the church on Saturdays, the halls and carpets humming with silence. Donning the cape, shield, sword, and muscular breastplate, Billy felt like his true self, the unseen seen, the spiritual made tangible. He liked to pray in the outfit, flat on the floor like a dead roach.

After several blocks, Billy turned his truck into Apple Creek, the newest subdivision of Limburg. The first house rose like a fort, a box of expensive brick that could have held four families, though Billy knew only three people lived there, the Boudinots. An old man was out walking a German Shepherd. Billy gave him a friendly wave, didn't recognize him. Must be a Catholic.

He wound around the streets until he could see the creek. The apple trees had long been ripped out, but when Billy was young they were the edge of town, a huge orchard stretching over and off into the horizon, rows and rows of jagged limbs laden with fat red orbs. There'd been pickings, hayrides, and mazes in the field. A celebration of the harvest.

Decades later, at a family reunion, Uncle Charlie revealed what else took place at Apple Creek. Billy always loved Uncle Charlie, the best storyteller in the family with a high-pitched laugh that shook his fat cheeks and turned heads across the room. After years away Billy had recently returned to Limburg as a pastor when Uncle Charlie told him about the edge of the field near the creek, where the men of the town used to gather in their hoods. "It's the funny thing 'bout apple trees," Uncle Charlie said, leaning across a picnic table, the scent of whiskey pouring from his breath. "They're short but damn if they're sturdy. It don't matter if he's two inches 'bove the ground or six feet in the air, he'll still dangle and kick 'til he chokes. They always choke in this town, Billy boy." Uncle Charlie winked and took another sip from his mug. Billy looked around at the other family, hoping someone else had heard. "What you looking for? They all know. I guess as pastor now you'll learn these things." Uncle Charlie giggled, wiped his forearm across his mouth, his eyes looking off over Billy's shoulder. "Yessir, boy, you'll know this town like you never thought you would."

Billy stopped his truck and looked out across the creek, now clear of all but a few trees, its waters bubbling between back porches, an above-ground pool, a bonfire pit. His crooked hands moved around the wheel without stopping. He wished he'd brought coffee, maybe some of his secret cigarettes. He needed something to do with his hands. His fingers rubbed the worn leather of the wheel and felt soothed. He'd come here to solidify his purpose and will for the task ahead. But sitting hunched in the truck, he felt old.

Billy thought about those Easter pageants, all the fake nails and outfits. But he'd seen the real thing, as a young man in the Philippines. There the crucifixion was real, suffering offered openly. Men allowed themselves to be nailed, whipped, hung for hours. He'd heard them cry out, marveled at the surprise in their eyes from the pain, how it transformed them. There the blood flowed brighter than any sunlight. And how had Billy lived his life after their examples? Mildly, and with nothing to show. Pulling the gearshift brought a new soreness to his fingers as Billy steered away and into a thin fog rolling through the streets of Limburg.

Billy's blue truck fit perfectly into its parking space, a plaque with his name designating the spot. He grabbed for the comb to fix his hair again. When the left side wouldn't stay down, Billy licked two fingers and pressed until most of the faint strands complied, wiped his hand on his jeans before climbing out of the cab. Rather than try to look executive by wearing a suit, Billy worked in a button-up and jeans. Appearing like a regular joe helped his pastoring, made him relatable.

Peaceful Valley Baptist Church was a low, long brick building, round bushes in pea gravel on either side of the front doors. Stained-glass windows dotted the wall facing the street, all beneath a towering steeple with chipping white paint that tore off in high winds and fell across the road like snow. Next to the road sat a sign with his name painted in black letters: "Reverend William Gadsen II." The changeable letters read:

SUNDAY SERMON
HABAKKUK 2 THE LORDS REPLY
HAPPY RETIREMENT PASTOR BILLY!
GOD BLESS!

He glanced at the plastic letters for a moment before unlocking and entering the front door.

His finger ran along the wood grain of the pews as he made his way to the altar and climbed the stairs to the stage. Billy loved coming into the sanctuary when no one else was at church. A buzz, a cool rush of air met him as he stood still at the pulpit and looked out over the cavernous room.

His father had taken Billy and his seven siblings to Peaceful Valley often. They grew up steeped in the language and the scents and the instinctual quiet breathing during prayers or Bible readings. His father would sit next to Billy with a tanned arm over the back of the pew, his father's hand sometimes resting on Billy's neck. His father had enormous arms with hair matching his mustache, deep black like crow's feathers. He and Billy fished along

Apple Creek. He'd taught Billy to play baseball and poker and to ride bikes all over the old poletown neighborhood of Limburg.

It was years later—more than a decade after his father bled out in a distant field, his leg mangled in a combine—that Billy learned the details of who his father was on Saturday nights. Why the neighborhood was named poletown. An old parishioner, Gordie Hahn, had called him to the South County VA Home, asked specifically for Billy from his deathbed. Gordie wanted a confession. Baptists didn't usually do final confessions, but Billy couldn't refuse a dying request.

When Billy arrived he found Gordie wasted away, his cheekbones nearly poking through the skin of his face. But Gordie's memory was clear as he told Billy about Saturday nights at Apple Creek. "Sometimes we was harmless, just bluffing and jawing." Gordie paused for a deep breath. He lay on his back, watched the ceiling as he spoke. "Other nights a man had to get his hands dirty. I done it once, and your dad, Old Bill, he done it lots of times. Old Bill was the one that supplied the poles. Why," Gordie reached his skeletal hand out, settled it over Billy's, "I remember you. Bill brought you around sometimes. You's too young to remember, but you was there too. You was there."

Billy had no memory of the meetings, had been far too young for inductions, but the thought of those church men hollering in a circle of night, his father's hands hammering a head onto a stick. The look on the head's face, how it must have changed with every slick thud. How the men must have laughed, the same men who wore the Easter pageant costumes. Who hammered plastic nails. Who brought down the whip. Who were practiced. Like his father.

Billy had gone to seminary up north. He'd been at protests, beaten by cops in 1968 Chicago. Traveled the world and his country. Walked broken alleys of America with his bare feet and then returned to Limburg not only a new man but—in Billy's vision—a new kind of man, a progressive his hometown had never envisioned. A silent fighter for the just cause. Billy lost twenty pounds during a hunger strike in the 80s over discriminatory zoning laws, his stomach caved in under his ribs, his skin sallow and green. He'd been heckled at town hall meetings, his tires slashed, his life threatened by scribbled notes left in his mailbox. Voting rights. Women's health. Discrimination in schools. Forty years of struggle.

Now, looking out on the stiff pews and tinted, dusty sunlight, Billy was overwhelmed with uselessness. Nothing had changed in forty years. His father had never changed, had likely been buried with his ideas intact, his murders unacknowledged, unknown to his own son, the blood passed down, hand to hand. The men about town were still the same. The very room was ageless. Billy imagined himself as a young boy stumbling into the sanctuary, his eyes on the long beams of the ceiling in wonder than anything could ever stay so high. It hadn't changed since he was a child, but the church seemed shrunked to Billy now. For forty years he had been hoping and working for change, for his faith to mean something. Now he placed his hopes in the gasoline.

Behind the church, on the far side of the dumpster lay scattered cigarette butts. The janitor mentioned them a few times, assumed they were left by some wandering teenagers. No one suspected Billy's small vice, the pack he kept in his desk and puffed on in the early mornings, a lingering habit and inheritance from his father. He gazed across the highway to a cornfield, each row perfectly straight, every leaf blindingly green. He remembered how his mother would slap his father's shoulder when he puffed smoke at the dining room light, his feet crossed and hands behind his head. Mother called it "un-Gospel behavior," but his father would grin and look satisfied, and eventually his mother would smile too. At night after dinner, Billy would watch the smoke curl around the yellow light of the bulb and think how close this was to God, fog and brilliance hovering over the family, billowing from his father's deeply stained teeth.

He tossed the filter onto the gravel and walked into his office, a quiet room with wood shelves and soft lamps. His back hurt as he settled in his chair. Billy rubbed the muscles with his fingers, which quickly became sore themselves. He stopped when he heard the door creak open. Jean, his volunteer secretary, poked her head in. "Brother Billy. Your back acting up again?" Jean worked three days a week. He'd hoped she wouldn't be in today, wanted the quiet.

"I'm fine, Jean, thank you. Do you need something?"

"Well," she took the question as an invitation to enter the room. Her hair was tightly permed, her back too straight as she took confident steps across the room. Billy appreciated her work ethic, but retired teachers were usually more trouble than aid. Shit-stirrers. "I took the liberty yesterday of picking out worship music for Sunday." She smiled and swatted her hand at him, tossed away his imagined gratitude. The sugary tone in Jean's voice brought Billy physical pain. "I was hoping to glance over your sermon and make sure I've matched the hymns."

"Habakkuk chapter two is the text, Jean."

"Yes, pastor, but what will you be addressing in the chapter?"

Billy flipped through a couple books on his desk. He wasn't sure which books or if he was even reading them. "I'm in the middle of that now. You know I'm often tweaking my sermon right up to Sunday morning." He stood and gave as sincere a smile as he could muster. "Don't worry. I'm sure the songs'll do fine. I appreciate it, Jean."

She nodded and visibly shivered, flashed her teeth. "No problem, pastor. At least you won't have to be up late tweaking sermons much longer." Her lipstick was a brilliant red. He wondered if she bit her lips. "Anything else you need from me?"

"No, you can go on home, Jean. There's nothing interesting going on today."

"Well you must have something interesting planned with all that gas in your truck bed." Hand to her hip, Jean raised an eyebrow.

"Laraine Jennings is sick and needs someone to mow her lawn. I told her I'd come over this afternoon."

"Quite a yard that Laraine has. What's an old woman need with three whole acres of fresh-cut grass? But that's kind of you. There's what you can do once you retire: Pastor Billy's Lawn Care. A good way to keep yourself young!" Jean laughed, moved to duck out of the room.

"Jean?"

"Yes Pastor?"

Billy collected images in his brain of all the good ones, the gentle hearts like Jean who had given him tiny shards of hope throughout the years. "Thank you."

"You're welcome." Jean paused, then waved and left. Billy rubbed his back and listened for the front door and then to Jean's car as she drove from the lot. He walked out to check the gas cans. Untouched. Billy glanced at his watch, decided to wait a few more hours.

The storage room smelled of mold. Billy worried the uniforms might have faded, but when he put the pieces on they looked as good as ever, the purple of the cape bright, shin-guards glistening like steel, the abs of the breastplate perfectly defined, if dusty. It was Billy that had soured. He moved toward a mirror on the back of the door. He'd lost two inches of height in the last ten years. The skin of his neck sagged, wrinkles and spots covering his face. His thin arms protruding out from the breastplate made Billy into an old tortoise. The one thing that hadn't left him was his vision. Billy could see himself clearly as ever. But what good was seeing alone? In the mirror he looked like a wise gentle leader, but he didn't feel it. Whatever his failings in body and life, Billy could still be a warrior.

The cape flapped as Billy whirled in front of the mirror. The costume helped. He took off the plastic pieces, wiped them down to clean any grime. He wanted the armor to sparkle. Billy carried the outfit back to his office, tossed the pieces in his chair and lowered himself to his knees, joints cracking with effort, a hand clasped to the desk for support. He needed every ounce of strength, which only came from humility. Billy lowered himself onto his stomach, down until his face was pressed into the sharp fibers of the carpet. Hands outstretched, fingers splayed, Billy wanted every inch of skin on the floor, pressed down hard enough to bleed. "Dirt," he whispered. "I am dirt." And he lay praying in harsh whispers for two hours, giving the many shops time to open and fill.

Billy drove his truck through the parking lot of the West County Mall, ten miles outside of Limburg. The centurion helmet scraped the top of the cab, causing Billy to huddle over the wheel. He noticed a few glances from passing cars, but they'd shaken their heads and kept on. He planned to begin at 11:30 with just enough people present to have an impact, the appropriate amount of witness. Ignoring a number of good parking spots, Billy drove over the curb of the sidewalk. His truck stopped in front of West County's main entrance, the automatic glass doors opening and closing in erratic confusion. Several exiting customers sidled around the grill of the truck, stared and quickly walked off.

Billy stumbled out of the cab and made sure the purple cape was clear before shutting the door. The skin of his calves looked soft and white against the silver shin guards and leather frock. He grabbed the gas cans, had to place the sword and shield under his arms to manage them all. The strength and balance required was almost too much, and he nearly fell with the first few steps, the rolling weight of the containers pulling him in every direction. His back strained, but Billy managed to walk down the main corridor of the mall and into the central plaza. A number of shoppers were watching now. A group of young kids laughed at the odd sight: an old man in plastic Roman armor too big for him, two heavy jugs sloshing and pulling on his arms, sweat running down his forehead and strands of white hair sticking to his skin.

Low chatter was building in the central plaza, some electricity in the air alerting people to drop their plastic bags and pay attention. Old ladies walking swiftly paused their gaits, jeweled hands moving to cover their mouths. Billy grunted with the strain of lifting the containers, but he managed to set the gas cans onto a food court table. He pulled from his pocket a few pages of notes, studied them.

The surrounding tables had been cleared of shoppers. A security guard stepped forward, waved at Billy as if to assess the danger. The man's belly spilled lightly over his belt, the pale skin of his cheeks too young to grow hair.

"Hey there, Grandpa. What is this? What's with the get up?" Billy couldn't hear through his helmet, lifted the bulky thing from his head and held it against his body. Sweat dripped down his forehead, stung his eyes. "Eh? What was that?"

The guard raised his voice. "What. Are you. Doing?"

"My job. The Macy's people sent me."

With a blank face, the guard walked off to a corner of the plaza, talking quickly on his walkie.

Billy dropped his helmet and laid his papers out on a table, some verses to mention, a short letter he'd composed. Watching the security guard march toward the Macy's, Billy cleared his throat and rapped sword against shield. He expected a metal ringing like the peal of a church bell. Instead the shield made a hard plastic thwack. But the sound managed to draw attention, and Billy spoke above the murmuring crowd.

"Excuse me, folks. Sorry to cause a stir. Could I have a moment of your time?" Eyes darted around. Billy used his best pastor's voice, all his decades of practice at work. "I'm a local minister here in the region, out of Limburg, and I have a message I was burdened to share with you."

Several shoppers nodded their heads and backed away, hoping to avoid the sorry type of fundamentalist street preachers that plagued malls.

" 'If anyone causes these little ones to stumble, it would be better for them if a large millstone were hung around their neck and they were thrown into the sea.' Are y'all familiar with that verse?" The crowd stiffened. Billy moved toward the gas cans, turned one of the caps. The echo of strollers and check-out machines and tired families could still be heard in farther parts of the building, but everything around Billy was silent. He leaned down and took a quick sniff of the gas. "Do y'all believe He means what He says?"

A woman screamed as Billy lifted the container and spilled it over his head, the smell pouring deeply into his nostrils, dribbling into his mouth despite his tightly held lips. Billy's arms shook, but as the gas fell in a steady stream—running down to pool on the floor—the can became lighter, and his shoulders relaxed as five gallons washed over him. Billy dropped the can next to him on the floor. His clothes were dripping, his eyes bloodshot. Billy wiped gas from his face and eyebrows, spit what had fallen into his mouth. He gazed at the table and grinned. He wouldn't need the second can.

People in the crowd shouted when Billy pulled the lighter from his pocket, the circle growing wider, some fleeing for the door as if he meant to bring the building down. A young woman covered her child's eyes, yelled "Oh God, don't do this, mister!" A low wailing carried through the plaza, people speaking rapidly with one another, some positioning themselves to stop him. But with his finger on the lighter, no one took the chance.

"They will say I was crazy. Depressed. A lost shepherd. Don't believe them. I do this for all of you." Billy spun around to face the entire circle, his pointed finger moving from individual to individual, making contact with their fearful eyes. Then he pointed at himself, resting his finger against the slick breastplate "As a prophet, as a warrior, I'm to speak God's truth to this world. I hope—with my death—to bring about what this life could not, a peace that passes all meaning or control."

Billy bowed his head. "Father, help me," he whispered. He didn't know which father he meant.

Loud screams rang through the entire mall now. Shoppers ran for the doors. Sirens rose in the distance. Three security guards were pushing back the crowds, dozens of cellphones lifted high and recording.

"Woe to him who builds a city with bloodshed and establishes a town by injustice!" Billy's voice rose and wavered with each line, the reverent, musical reading style of his childhood, sitting on the pews next to his father, held by an arm made solid from the work of the farm. "The Lord has determined that the people's labor is only fuel for the fire, that the nations exhaust themselves for nothing. For the earth will be filled with the knowledge of the Lord as the waters cover the sea." A small flame flickered from the lighter. Billy dropped it at his feet.

The first sensation was a burst of air, the heat rising swiftly followed by a roar. When the flames erupted several men rushed at Billy, but the fire pulsed so quickly through his clothes and hair and skin, the men stopped short of his body, a black and glowing pillar, thin and erect, as straight and still as Billy had ever stood in his life. He wanted them to see him as he had dreamed, a holy warrior adorned by the fire.

The plastic centurion pieces melted and dribbled around his limbs. He resisted the urge to collapse to the ground, kept his mind occupied. Billy squinted at the ceiling over the plaza, windows allowing sunlight to filter down in square shafts. Billy could make out smoke swirling in the light, and he was taken back to his father smoking at the dinner table, his mother protesting faintly. Billy's mother would sometimes say "If you're smoking in this house, you better be on fire." They'd all laughed, his father breathless and slapping the table with his palm.

Billy hoped he'd open his eyes and be back at that table, his father and mother relaxing after dinner, his father pulling smoke into his lungs as the end of the cigarette crackled and fog swirled up like holy spirits. He hoped everyone ended up in the same place.

TRAINS

My boyfriend and I found an impossibly cheap apartment with large windows. Cathedral windows, the landlord called them. We both cringed at that, but the light flooding the living room in the morning did have the look of the sacred. The kitchen was long and open with beautiful subway tile. Thick lacquer gave the black cabinets a professional glow. Of course, there was a catch: a few feet outside the windows were a set of tracks, frequented by hulking trains.

We almost didn't take the place. We'd just moved to a new city for my boyfriend's job, a great career step for a young journalist but with little money. I'd been unemployed for six months, searching for work in advertising, writing copy for some obscure company that sold European clothes or lawnmowers or band aids. At least that's what I told my boyfriend, Gregory. The reality was I'd stopped looking after so many unreturned emails. My desktop was loaded with dozens of resume versions. I didn't know what I wanted to do, just looking to contribute somehow. It was more of a feeling. In those awkward Skype interviews I wanted to pour myself out to the pixelated faces: "I can do anything if you'll give me the chance to care." During an internet lag in one interview I said as much out loud, hoping the idea would carry through the wires and waves without the words. Turns out they heard, began scribbling with sour faces that shone clear through the grainy screen. I didn't get the job. Or the fifteen after. Eventually I quit applying, made up elaborate days spent filling out forms, networking in coffee shops around the city. Gregory never fished for details, just said "you'll get something" before turning a page in whatever novel he was reading. He rarely discussed his own work, a crime reporter for the main city paper. We were content remaining mysterious to each other.

Gregory thought the trains would be too much, that the noise would psychologically damage us. He imagined our muscles constantly tensed, unable to relax in our own home. But looking around taught us we—meaning Gregory—couldn't afford better. So the next week we moved in our dishes, our couch, our little row of succulents. We weren't sure how we would react to a hundred tons of speeding steel on the other side of the wall. Bricks normally appear sturdy, but the walls of our new apartment seemed flimsy with the tracks easily visible from those grand windows. Gregory hefted a box of books, set them down on the kitchen counter. "How is this even legal? Aren't there codes to prevent this kind of thing?" Still, we tried not to worry until something actually roared by.

The tracks were not used by commuter trains. No sleek silver bullets. The tracks were designed for commercial freights, rusted boxes of steel hauling oil or lumber or minerals, their hides covered in intricate graffiti. The landlord was honest with us: these trains were not quiet. They were not going to silence their horns near the building. Rather, the landlord warned us the horns blasted as they approached. I imagined the conductor, a tired, bored man with overalls stretched across his paunch, gathering sadistic joy from his horn, breaking up our days, forcing us to stop and notice.

The first train came through while I was washing dishes. I'd scrubbed the same plates three days ago, before packing them into boxes. But Gregory was convinced that dust had coated them on the journey, so every single dish we owned needed to be washed again before being arranged in the cabinets. Water in the sink formed the tiniest ripples seconds before the sound hit my ears, all-encompassing, like listening underwater. The noise moved in waves, steadily more forceful until I could see the train, a shadow of gears and iron between flashes of light. Squeaking wheels added a randomness to the percussive clacking of the cars, each ticking by with a steady rhythm. As the sound faded, Gregory stuck his head out of the bedroom. "That wasn't so bad." We smiled, happy to have gotten away with it all.

Two more trains came that first day. One arrived during a moment of rest. I'd stopped unpacking to scroll through Twitter. The train passed with incredible speed and no horn, a dark flicker in the window followed by rumbling that shook the building. But the distraction got me up and working again. Later in the evening Gregory and I began fighting about something as inconsequential as where to place the succulents. We weren't looking to hurt each other. But the pressurized tension of the move had to be released somehow. Just as the angry statements were subsiding and adequately apologized for another train blew through, this time a horn sounding the entire way. We immediately grabbed each other, furiously made out. It didn't develop any further as we were both sweaty and surrounded by our lives in need of arranging. But the moment was a nice way to christen a new place.

The first night was the greatest, deepest sleep I have ever known. My dreams were lolled on the light memory that freights moved a mere fifteen feet from our vulnerable, sleeping brains. But the trains did not disturb us. Instead they left a light, floating impression of sound, like living near the sea.

Over the next several weeks we discovered their erratic intervals. We might go hours without hearing one, then suddenly three in fifteen minutes, moving in opposite directions on the same track. I would stand close to the window, sparks blinking off the wheels, and wonder how they passed through each other, how there had not been a collision. I thought about this great beast, a thing from another time, growling outside my window. If I opened the window and leaned I could have touched it. It traveled fast enough to take my arm off.

Something in the train relaxed me, a low-level positive beam. Similar to the antidepressants I used to swallow but without clear-cutting every emotion. I'd wake up motivated, started applying all over town. I determined to fulfill all those lies I'd been telling Gregory, sending resumes and meeting contacts. He was more buoyant too, his energy high even when staying up all night covering the latest bout of violence.

I began to watch the trains more instead of just listening. Often they were streams of black tanks concealing some dangerous liquid. Sometimes they were enormous bins of coal or wheat, even stacks of imported cars. The only person visible was the conductor, though I could never be sure exactly who he was. When I heard an approaching train I pressed against the cathedral windows but caught only a vague glimpse of him, an impression of a human being. He was old, a white beard flowing down the side of the engine. Or so I thought. Was he happy? Did he love his job? Did he know his effect, how these trains were changing us? I attempted to draw him but came away with vague scratches. I had never been a talented artist, which would have been convenient. A better reason for sloth. Was it even the same conductor? I assumed this logically impossible, yet there he was every time, the whisper of a smile and a white beard blowing past us.

The trains did interrupt movies and TV shows. At first we would pause and wait for them to pass before recalling who was trying to kill who. But eventually we accepted the noise as a kind of contribution, a way to emphasize emotional crescendos or skip over useless dialogue. These moments became fate, part of the universe's design.

The trains intensified sex. The first time we fucked in the apartment, Gregory and I laid back afterward and stared at the ceiling, each of us breathless, emptied and unwound. While the world flashed swiftly just outside the window in thunderous noise, we were moving with each other, our own sound absorbed in the music of the train. We began to hold back, try not to come before the train's arrival, wanting some auditory parallel with our own. We were disappointed when the alignment didn't work. Eventually sex felt more about the train, our attention only half on the other person's body, our ears piqued and desperately listening for some roar far off in the distance.

My networking coffees dried up. I spent less and less time searching for work. The majority of my day was in front of our massive windows, occupying myself there in order to be present, to witness the trains. I read books in an uncomfortable corner, overwatered the succulents. All to be closer to this phenomenon we had absorbed, the conductor, the light and sound and low re-verberations he brought. I grew suspicious, imagined it all differently. Was it scheduled with us, the way the trains came at perfect moments, giving form to our lives? Or were we shaping around them, molding ourselves to fit the trains?

I invented stories about where they were going, what all the cargo was for. How the conductor spent his Saturdays. The tracks sped east for a time before suddenly diverting south, continuing past the border, over the Panama Canal, through the Amazon, down to Tierra del Fuego. This is where the conductor lived. Every week he traversed two continents, bringing mercury and sulfuric acid and liquid nitrogen to scientists, delivering danger to keep us all safe and ticking. On Saturdays he sat out on a bluff overlooking the ocean spray, sipped beer and lounged in his chair, let the waves lull him to sleep.

Sometimes the conductor came from India, traversed the arctic ice sheet. Sometimes he delivered live animals, mythical creatures that beat their wings and clawed at the edges of their containers. He was 200 years old, driving them since the first trains. Born with them. The stories were infinite, a way to pass time while I waited for the real thing to come by. All the little games you play with yourself to stay alive.

My phone vibrated against the kitchen counter. It was hours later that I picked it up and listened to the voicemail. One of the networking contacts had come through. I was offered a job, marketing for a local environmental advocacy group. The pay was decent, the work gratifying. But as the voicemail ended my fingers moved on their own, deleted the message and set the phone down. I watched the floor for a moment, unsure what was happening. Then I returned to my corner, the uncomfortable reading nook against those great, glorious windows that let a little too much light in.

The weight difference between a train and a car is like an elephant crushing a soda can. The front grill of the engine is called the pilot, also known as the cowcatcher. This prevents an animal or person—when struck—from crunching beneath the wheels, causing derailment. Instead the body is flung upward, sailing in the air, twitching above the cars as they safely pass.

The trains continued to pulse through our lives, though we were living them apart. Gregory was busy chasing the latest crime statistics at all hours. I spent more and more time watching, feeling the rhythm of the cars through the wood floors, up my legs and into the rest of me. A buzzing sensation carried to the bone. I'd briefly been telling him the truth, pursuing real employment. But it was back to lying again, quick snippets about applications, promising leads, interviews. Gregory would sigh and say "It's okay. You don't have to feel bad. I know it's tough out there."

Several months into the lease the landlord slipped a note under the door. The trains would be stopping. Someone had been in violation of safety codes, the builders or the transport companies. Lawyers had gotten involved. It was decided that traffic would be diverted to another line. We read the letter together. At the bottom was a short paragraph explaining that—what with the unsightly locomotives out of the picture—the rent would soon be raised.

We decided to break our lease, move out immediately. While packing our things, Gregory asked me why I didn't take the environmental advocacy job. He'd run into the contact at a bakery, been questioned about it. "What have you been doing all this time?" His neck turned red and splotchy. But I had no clear answer, just looked out the window, tried to keep all the muscles and skin of my face still. The succulents were all in a row, long dead, rotten shadows of their old selves. Tears rippled at the edge of Gregory's eyes. But he never liked to cry, pulled them back into their ducts. He began arranging his own things, separately and with care.

I couldn't stay in the apartment. Besides not affording the new rent, the walls radiated silence that felt heavy on the skin. I missed them both. I missed it all, wondered what had really become of me as I shut the door to the place for the last time. They really were fantastic windows.

Since then I've been couch surfing, counting on the generosity of old friends until it runs out. Lying on beat up sofas and air mattresses and blankets stretched across a floor. Sleep is hard to come by, but when I do the dreams are vivid. The conductor is coming for me, a wisp of beard covering him like a dark cloud. I'm on the tracks, struck and lifted high by the cowcatcher, but it's not painful at all. It's a beautiful sight, an enormous line of cars like a rope leading into the past, stretching off and over the horizon.

UNCLE BOB

Uncle Bob's ass was clean enough. I snapped off the latex gloves and dropped them into an orange wastebasket. Bob wriggled face-down, trying to turn his head, the skin on his neck stretching like a water balloon as the support chains of his Hoyer lift pulled taut. "You sure do take your time, Danny Boy." He slurred the S. Bob rarely put his teeth in anymore.

"You sure do shit a lot, Uncle Bob. Next time I'll leave you sit-ting in it. How long you think before the nurse changes you?" I grabbed an oversized diaper from the bedside dresser. Yellow light seeped through the blinds and made the sheets look sour.

"They'd let me ride out until the weekend, I expect. If I'm be-ing surly."

I stretched the diaper under him, secured the Velcro and pulled his pants up, careful not to brush the stump of Bob's left leg, lost to diabetes. "Or longer. Can't blame them. So you can either say 'thank you' or shut the fuck up about it. You feel like a smoke?"

"*Thank you,*" he said with gusto. Red stubble covered most of his face. He was pleased with his reply, always a comedian.

I spun the crank of Uncle Bob's lift, hoisted and twisted him toward his wheelchair, his back straining against the supports and chains. He licked his lips as I lowered him to the seat. The chair shook while he huffed, sighed, settled in.

I stopped by every Monday and Wednesday. Uncle Bob couldn't afford a quality nursing home, so he made do with the shuffling Medicare ladies of the Cypress Creek County Retirement Facility. He didn't fit in with the other thin-haired, dementia-ed patients mumbling up and down the halls, though Bob wasn't exactly spry. Time and hard living had chipped at him, hairy and sagging like a moldy peach.

With an electric whir, Uncle Bob aimed his chair at the door. "Why's a young guy like you coming to see a fart like me?" He smacked his gums together.

I was furiously washing my hands at the sink. "I can't have people gossiping around town about you rolling around in your own filth."

"They've said worse things about the family. Let 'em cluck. For Christsake, Danny, go live a little. And bring my smokes."

I looked at him in the mirror. Go live a little.

Bob was the first person I should have told. The one person. But I couldn't confess to my uncle how I'd soon be making the family plunge, how it was just across the parking lot, Dad's old revolver hidden in the glove compartment. It'd looked deeply familiar in the shoebox that morning, felt like ice on my palm.

I grabbed Bob's pack off the dresser and followed him out the door. "You shouldn't smoke these." The hallway was humid with the faint smell of urine.

"Yes I should." Uncle Bob's wheels spiraled down the hallway.

I fast-walked to catch up and tossed the Marlboros into Bob's lap. "Here. I need to go to work."

Bob's eyes never left his goal, the back door opening to a small concrete square. The thick air made his cheeks pink. "Yeah, you got all kinds of shit to do. Mr. Responsible, looking out for me. Go on, then. See you Wednesday."

I stopped walking, and Uncle Bob stopped wheeling. He winked at me before clutching his Marlboros and rolling out the door.

✠

From the moment Great-Grandpa Jeffrey stepped up to his rafter, the rest of the McKays were marked for failure. We hold the unofficial county record for attempted suicides, something we're loath to discuss when pressed about it in the Co-op or the liquor store. We don't like the details getting out, how Jeffrey, his sorghum and rye having washed away in the floods of '15 and '16, climbed onto his dining room table, fashioned a noose from his carpenter's belt, placed it around his neck, and jumped. As his children slept, Jeffrey swung through the dusty air of his dining room. His belt snapped and he collapsed onto the corner of the oak table. It was Cal, my Grandpa, who heard the wet thud, who paddled down the stairs to find his father twitching on the floor, who was left to ponder the bloody table and the broken strip of leather dangling from the ceiling. Jeffrey recovered with nothing but a dent above his ear. Twelve years later, Cal swallowed a bottle of pills. He woke up three days later with slurred speech.

If you do happen to get a McKay—a cousin once removed, perhaps—talking about our history, she'll smile to herself and admire what quitters we are. Jim McKay lit his barn up from the inside, eventually diving out of the loft. He scorched eighty percent of his skin and spent the rest of his life in a hospital bed being spoon-fed by his wife. Cousin Doug dropped off the Whitewater Bridge and nearly drowned. He came to on the bank a few hours later and walked the half mile to his kid's tee-ball game, sat on the bleachers in his sopping clothes. Great-Aunt Ruth hoped to crush her skull under her husband's tractor. She rose early and hid beneath the rusted axle, her nose touching the rubber of the tires, smelling mud set into the treads. Her husband lumbered into the cab, turned the key, and threw the tractor in reverse to attach his combine. He looked down as soggy Aunt Ruth wiped off her dress and marched inside to make coffee. In a family where almost everyone tried to off themselves, only one made it.

That'd be my dad, Mitch. Mom was locked in an Illinois pen for cooking crystal. That afternoon I was at a gas station swiping Sudafed when Dad fell back on tradition. But unlike every other McKay, Dad didn't hesitate. One decisive twitch of a finger changed five generations of history. Years later, people around town talked about Dad like a hero, like some legendary ballplayer—the guy who made it out. But he didn't look so heroic when I walked in to him splattered across the living room wall. I sat on the sofa and stared into the dark-red carpet, tried to mimic the look on half of Dad's face. The same scowl he gave me when I came home at night, my eyes bleary and pink. He could have been thinking of me. Uncle Bob found me there, making that face. He grabbed my neck and took me to his cabin.

✠

I drove to work. Chemical powder flaked off the jumpers of the factory workers, their faces obscured by goggles and helmets. They ambled past the guard shack, throwing up half-hearted waves without lifting their heads. I stood up to watch the 7:00 PM shift change, my arms stretching from one wall to the other, wasting my life in a six-by-six foot hut so the Nihikawa Chemical Company could cover their asses. Insurance purposes. They manufactured high fructose corn syrup, monoglyceride, other snack-cake chemicals. Watching the shift change was the active part of the job.

I was drawn to the suicide rate. At least three line workers every year, and usually one management. Suspicion buzzed around the factory, a darting of the eyes, a who's-going-to-kick-the-next-bucket electricity that felt dangerous and familiar. I would have fit in, if I ever left the guard shack. I sat in a chair and radioed trailer numbers to the shipping station. The trailers sat across a dust field with carbon-spewing towers behind them. Most Nihikawa trailers went through the Rainbow Bros. Trucking Company.

I felt bad for the brothers, for their awful name and childhood: "This is Brandon Rainbow. This is Theo Rainbow. And this here—with the crossed eyes—is little Jerry Rainbow." No kid can be blamed for his last name, but I imagined the children of the Rainbow family got their asses kicked in school. Toughened their faces. Hardened their bones.

The Rainbow in the company name took over the side of their trailers, the rest rendered in small print and all in colorless black. The brothers flaunted their bad luck, challenging the universe to flip them some good karma. They owned a trucking company, so I guess it worked. My job was oppressive, being confined alone to a cell at the factory gate, but it was the rows of tall, black Rainbows with attached serial numbers that really numbed my brain. "Rainbow HJQX–5703–9468. Rainbow SPVW–2169–4407." The numbers would flash at random, eating a bagel or sitting in the stands at a football game. "Rainbow DTCZ–4483–9271." I'd whisper trailer numbers in my sleep until Sheila jabbed me with an elbow.

Daphne left some time ago. Jody, way before that. But Sheila—with her maroon lipstick and three-inch heels—had been around awhile, two years at least. There'd been some good times, quiet nights eating soup in bed, parties at her cousin's farm where we'd guzzle peach schnapps. Sheila had been clean for years, but she'd gone on a bender last month, slashed couch cushions, ripped out vent covers, pointed with a knife, taken a stab at me. She disappeared for two weeks until the 2:00 AM call from the sheriff, her body found strung out, cold and bloated in a ditch. I thanked the sheriff, stumbled into the kitchen, pulled down a bottle and didn't stop. I loved Sheila. I knew I should have sobbed, but I never was much on grieving. The only thing in my brain was a number, "Rainbow LDCP–4955–6025," though it faded and changed with the drink.

In the back of my mind I'd always considered suicide, learned the suddenness of it at a young age with Dad. I'd heard stories about family attempts at reunions, though never from Uncle Bob. He hated the stereotypes, hated his brother. Hated me for being left to take care of.

Uncle Bob was the McKay everyone wanted to see die. He'd always been a fat, violent drunk. Riding with him as a kid, he'd pull over into a ditch and pretend to give driving lessons as he slept off his Old Crow. Bob lost his leg a few years after Dad died. I'd moved into the spare room of his cabin, an old hunting lodge made of molding logs. He was sympathetic at first, made me hash browns for breakfast with sorghum on toast. He even went sober for a time, took me fishing every afternoon. But a couple months in I came home to bottles on the floor and no Bob. He was rough after that.

Bob worked at the fireworks warehouse out by the Interstate. He'd sit there for hours sipping whiskey and gorging on white donuts that dusted his beard with powder. Wheeling down the long aisles of the warehouse must have felt like the Vegas strip, explosive boxes with colorful ads like "Annihilator," "Widow Maker," or "Grim Reaper." The county waited to hear about Bob. He was an angry McKay, surrounded by thousands of pounds of explosives, with at least two guns on his chair. And he was Dad's brother. Expectations were high.

But through all the years in a wheelchair, all the drinks and diapers and dead family and a deadbeat nephew who stole from his medicine cabinet, Uncle Bob never even hinted at offing himself. Out of spite, probably.

✠

At first I considered the train, the quiet dignity of standing straight, facing down a foghorned light. But I could too easily chicken out, take five steps to the left and have to live with myself. A car wreck was no sure thing. Burning was painful and contemplative. Drowning had the same problems. I needed something swift. Zero reflection. I briefly settled on an explosion, something theatrical. But I couldn't access enough Ammonium Nitrate, so I dragged out Dad's gun. The same gun seemed fitting. The county would talk.

Clocking out of my shift, I walked through thick, red light—past rows of black Rainbow Bros.—to my car. I passed two more trucks before arriving home, grabbing the gun out of the glove box. A package had been wedged in the corner of my doorframe. Carrying the small box with both hands, I weaved around the center of the front room, a blank space in the carpet that would have been Dad. I'd moved into the old house at eighteen. The couch was a mess of crumbs that gathered in the slashes Sheila had cut. I unwrapped the package of bullets and placed the gun on the table. Turning it under the lamplight, Dad's revolver felt cold and awkward. Keeping it straight took practice. I aimed at the wall, put the barrel to my temple, whispered *pow*.

Grabbing a few of Sheila's bottles, I headed for the backyard. Mushrooms sprouted in diagonal lines across the tall grass. They made a wet rubber squeak as I kicked them on my way to the tree line. The bottle leaning against a trunk, I took twenty paces back, turned and looked, moved forward five paces. If I could hit a bottle from this distance, I could sure as shit split my own melon. My eyes lined the bottle to the sight as I dug my feet into the dirt, prepped for the recoil.

A hard pull on the trigger, the decisive flick I imagined Dad used. No thinking required.

An otherworldly vision, like someone else shot the bottle, like watching glass explode in a movie, pieces splashing against tree trunks and leaves. It was over before I expected. Pleased, I walked over to inspect the damage. Severe and total, shards glittering in a wide circle of debris, wider than Dad's. I was drawn to the label, a tattered shred of paper on the grass.

Old Crow. Uncle Bob's drink of choice.

We'd had our rocky times, him raging drunk through the cabin. But he'd taken me in, raised me in his way. He wasn't close to anyone except me. His only other visitors were church types trying to wrangle the old bastard into the flock. When I was gone, he'd be alone.

My legs cramped as I flipped the safety on before popping out the cylinder, the leftover bullets ringing against their chambers then hitting the dirt with a final, blunt sound.

I tossed the hollow gun onto the kitchen table, slumped into a chair and twirled the revolver around. Spinning it scratched the table varnish, flakes of cheap lacquer blowing off the edge and snowing to the floor. Even without bullets, the spinning felt dangerous and powerful. I still had the Old Crow label in my hand, crumpled it up and threw it into the sink, my elbow in perfect jump-shot alignment, like Uncle Bob taught me.

Uncle Bob had stopped me before I'd even started. We had a connection, however tricky. Our last meeting hadn't ended on much of a going-out note. In a sense, Bob's asshole demeanor made it easier to think about my own splatter. It wasn't enough to hang on to, but he deserved at least an ounce of respect. I spun the gun again. The barrel pointed to Sheila's toaster.

Wednesday there'd be a real goodbye. I'd thank Uncle Bob with a bottle of Old Crow, exit with some grace. I hid the gun in a ripped couch cushion. Two more days of staring down black rainbows, of diapers and cold Sheila and Dad staining the ceiling and pooling all over the floor. Two days. The gun was motivation. I could survive anything if I knew I'd never have to do it again.

✠

No other stench is quite like a nursing home in summer. I could never prepare myself for it, made my eyes itch. Walking down the Cypress Creek hall on Wednesday, past all those drooping faces, a different scent hit me. Something rosy, sickly sweet. Turning in the door, I saw Bob—more moldy than usual—speaking with a tall woman in a red pantsuit. They didn't notice me.

Uncle Bob snorted. "That'd be the day, Sister. That'd be the goddamn day. It's been a rough one, so get the fuck out."

She backed up a bit, gulped and straightened her suit. "Well, Robert, you got that much right. That will be the day the Lord sends sinners to the fiery dusts of eternal damnation to be alone forever. And you don't want that, honey. Nuh-uh. You sure don't."

Bob raised his head to narrow his eyes at the sister. "You won't be there, will you? I wouldn't mind a little lonely damnation. This place is close enough to a fiery pit. Why don't you go peddle lies down the hall. Convince those Gertrudes and Annabelles that don't know their bread pudding from their shit. Those old gals are looking for a holy b'jesus miracle," Bob wavered his voice, like a

TV preacher. "Sanctified! Them bitches are sanctified!" He closed his eyes, shook his hands in the air.

"Well," her large smile flattened. "I thought I'd cheer you up before visiting my Granny Sybil, but I see there's no open door to company here." She ducked out of the room, wiping mascara as she left.

Bob's eyes followed her out the door, to me. "Hell in a dick-sack. Why are you late?" Bob wheeled over by the window.

"Why do you always have to be such a jackass?" I moved into the room, toward the dresser, reaching for the gloves. I already regretted the visit.

"She's been coming in last couple of weeks and preaching at all the folks. Annoying, puffed-up Tammy Faye," Uncle Bob sighed. "But she passes time."

"Sure. You alright otherwise? You need to get cleaned up?"

Bob focused on the window though he couldn't see out through the folded-down blinds. He scratched a bushy eyebrow, then his ear. "They took my smokes away. Bothering the asthma patients or some shit."

Cigarettes seemed trivial next to the gun in my cushion. "Sounds rough, Uncle Bob. Come on over to the lift."

"Smokes was about all I had. I don't have much more than that." Bob moved a hand down to his missing leg. "I've been thinking about your old man lately. About Mitch." A long-dead house plant sat under the window. Bob picked at it. "Maybe he had the right idea. Maybe the whole damn family should've been doing it for real instead of half-assing it every time." He smacked his gums. "If I could go back, Danny. If I just had my leg again."

I was only half listening as I cranked the lift. "You'd do what?"

Bob opened his mouth, but closed it without a word.

The goodbye had been a mistake. Uncle Bob wasn't worth paying respects, and I'd left the Old Crow at home. I decided to skip work and pull out the gun as soon as I was through at the nursing home. "Come on, Uncle Bob. Out with it. I need to keep this short today."

"I'd've shot my fucking face off. Way back ago. I know I always been down on the family. But it's too much sometimes, Danny Boy. Heavy."

"You'd have followed the family?" My head snapped up. We locked eyes. Uncle Bob looked soft, pleading.

"I had plans to. Mitch and me were always talking about it. Working out the different ways."

I'd hoped for the normal, cantankerous Bob. Here he was being confessional, cutting my last, thin thread of respect for him. I leaned down and grabbed the sides of Bob's chair. He stank. "What about the shit you always said about Dad? 'Fucking crybaby?' 'Loser couldn't stake it.' You think I don't remember all that?"

"I know I said some of the wrong things—"

"All that shit you said about the family?" I was breathing huge gulps that still weren't enough. This wasn't the man I knew. Uncle Bob had taken care of me, hated me sometimes and all the while had wanted to be a real McKay, to follow Dad.

"Danny—"

"So why didn't you? Why not off yourself years ago?"

Uncle Bob looked down at his hands. "I was thinking about you." He'd been as suicidal as the rest of the damn family for years, waiting for me while I waited for him.

"You dumb bastard."

"I did it for you."

I turned around, raised my voice. "Yeah, and I did it for you! I had it ready. Right here." I formed my hand into a gun, put it to my temple. My finger trembled, heat coming off my face.

"What are you—Danny?"

"Go fuck yourself, Uncle Bob. You should have died years ago." Before he could respond, I bolted from the room. I'd driven almost two fathers to killing themselves, dropped them like hailstones. I found it harder than ever to live, wasn't even sure I could wait to get home, to the gun.

Stomping out past the tremoring old nightgowns, I hit the humid air. Slamming the car door, my hands clenched and twisted around the steering wheel, my eyes gushing quiet drops as I thought of Dad, tried again to mimic his face, that final look that found me every night I managed to sleep.

✠

Trees nearly covered the street to the Nihikawa Plant, breaking in quick flashes from shadow to disorienting light, like a film projector shining in my face. I hadn't meant to drive that direction. Just programmed routine. I kept squinting at the road.

That old, fat fuck. I'd always known about his pride, seen it sparkle at his cabin during poker games. The skin of his face would reflect a sallow white when he won, pink when he lost. Bob always thought highly of himself. He'd never seriously mentioned suicide before, always making jokes and turning our family history into a vaudeville play. He was the black sheep McKay, a quality I depended on. Hell, even admired sometimes. But wanting to off himself, and for years. He'd been stringing me along again, teaching me to drive while he drooled in the passenger seat. He was too chicken shit to do it.

If not for Bob, I could've shot myself years ago.

The plant parking lot had a sharp turn. Gunning the motor, I flew through the tiny gate arm, heard it crash over the hood, bang the trunk and fall away. The V6 engine sputtered, oscillating with cheap power. Large signs on the factory yard trailers flew past in black glints. Rainbow. Rainbow. I hit the gas harder.

I was in a narrow alley between plant sectors. I could see helmets in the windows, heard a siren off in the distance. Fifty feet ahead, a truck backed out of the loading dock. The wheels squeaked as I slammed the brake, more a reflex than a decision. Debris from the backseat flew forward. Styrofoam cups, paper bags, a phonebook hung in the air, all silhouetted again the freight, those black words that bore down with a force I couldn't control, washing over me with metal and dark sound. I finally had the face right.

✠

I opened one eye to the white pocks of suspended ceiling tiles, tried sitting up.

"Uncle Bob, I can't move."

"It's okay, kiddo." He hadn't called me that since before Dad died. "You're in half a body cast. You don't have a lot of wiggle room. Here." I heard the sharp S sounds in his voice, then the electric whir. He raised my head and placed a firm pillow underneath. The room looked like Uncle Bob's only bright and new, the bed with gizmos and buttons.

Uncle Bob's teeth were securely in his mouth, though a little brown. He'd shaved his beard, exposed his whiskey-ed cheeks to the air. Fluorescent lighting showed every wrinkle. The grey dress pants he only wore to family funerals. "I'm glad you're okay."

"You call this okay?" I glanced down my body to the cast, several inches of molded clay covering my hips and torso. A patch over my left eye, a sling for my left arm.

He rubbed his cheek, shrugged, and placed a hand over his good leg. "You look alive to me."

"You were going to kill yourself. Years ago." I used a harsh tone that startled him.

"Yeah. I was."

"Even though you hated Dad for doing it? Were you jealous?"

"Probably, yeah."

"So what's stopping you? You lost a leg. You live in a shitty home. No real family. Even I hate your guts. Why don't you flop down on the highway?" My voice peaked. A nurse ducked her head in and ducked out.

Uncle Bob cowered in his chair, his head shivering like he had a five-pound bag on his skull. "You're still here." Uncle Bob—the mean, one-legged drunk who used to kick my ass sitting down—sniffed, moaned, and sobbed. "You're all I got to go on, kiddo. You're all I'm living for."

I flinched when Uncle Bob laid one of his arms across my chest while the other rested on his stump for balance.

"I ain't going anywhere, Danny Boy. I'll sit here in this chair long as you need me." A string of snot dangled from his nose. He grabbed my hand and laid his face on my arm.

Even in his grief, the old guy was crafty. We had a suicide stand-off. No one could kill himself without condemning the other. I hesitated, angry at the responsibility of it all. My own life was one thing, but Uncle Bob's life—pathetic as he had it—was not something I could trifle with. Maybe that's why we had so many fucked-up suicides in the family, that last-second flash of obligation—maybe even love—saving them all in horrific ways. Except for Dad. Maybe that's why Bob resented Mitch, resented me.

I did the right thing in the moment, wrapped my good arm around Bob's shoulders and squeezed back. But I couldn't promise Uncle Bob I wouldn't do it, that I wasn't still waiting for the revolver stuffed in the tear of my sofa cushion. Bob wasn't enough to keep me alive. But I was enough for Uncle Bob. I didn't know how long that would last.

YOU'RE BEAUTIFUL

After her husband Henry died, Gladys lived alone. She kept the same house in the same way, full of food and free of dust. She stuck an insulin needle into her stomach every day at 4:00. The basement stairs gave her trouble, but Henry helped every so often, when he was feeling up to it. She made his favorite every Friday, smoked sausages with barbecue sauce and sauerkraut. Henry ate the sausage in three huge bites but savored the sauerkraut. 'Give her a can opener and in ten minutes you'll have a meal for a king,' he would say to the room.

Her children came by intermittently, but they were distracted, shaking their heads at her with droplets on their lids and never staying very long. Henry hid in the bedroom when they arrived. She wondered why this was. When he wasn't eating, Henry sat in a musty recliner and watched her, his face lean and smiling and his eyes so wide and no matter how many long minutes she peered back Henry never blinked.

At night she woke up in the dark and prayed until she fell asleep and in the morning she prayed again the same prayer. When she passed by a mirror she looked so beautiful and started giggling. 'You're beautiful,' Henry told her. She prayed about it.

In the evenings he scared her, the red sun hollowing his face. He'd stopped talking after a few weeks, just watched her with that grin. She began to creep around him. The sweat gleaming on his forehead made her worry and she felt like he would pounce at any moment, his fingers coiled on the arm of the chair.

147

One day she grabbed a pencil and shoved it into his eye. He kept smiling, stretched his lips even wider. She stabbed Henry's other eye and twirled the pencil around, colored both until they were nothing but grey holes, the lids ripped out like little strips of paper. She bent down to his face, looked through his eyes. Her lip trembled and she whispered like a prayer, 'You're beautiful.'

SIN EATERS

I wake up this morning like normal with my body in the bed but not like normal with my lower jaw flopped onto the floor. It's not detached, just stretched to some crazy length. I can see my lower lip with that rotten tooth behind it lying on the floorboards like a forgotten shoe. How it stays that way without breaking off I couldn't tell you. I touch the jaw with a finger, all the extra skin. There's no pain. Just a strange, sparkling weirdness. Getting dressed is a struggle since everything has to get around the jaw. Once I start moving, the thing becomes sore. I grab a scarf out the closet and try to pull everything back. All that skin bunches up but I manage to get the scarf around my head and tied off under the chin.

What's really strange about the jaw is the timing, Levi being put away just last week. I've hardly slept a wink since, lie most of the night gawking at the ceiling. I think crazy thoughts, wonder what kind of horribleness Levi must be witnessing at that exact moment, how he'll never be the same when he gets out. This morning a bit of gray light was peeking through the window when I finally nodded off, and I know my face was normal then. How a jaw sinks that way in a matter of hours, I haven't a clue.

I decide to get myself to Doc Parry, that dentist downtown. He's a kook but when you're holding your face together you go with close. Stepping out of the house I start to wake up and realize what a peculiar jam I'm in, so I hurry down the front steps to the sidewalk. I'm hitting a good stride when Eli, he's my neighbor and a Christian Scientist—which isn't near as interesting as it sounds—he sees me walking down the block holding my jaw in place and says, "Geraldine, where you going with that busted jaw? That grandson pop you again?" I try to reply with a "No, he's just been put back in the pen. This ain't but a toothache," but it ends all mangled and squirrely. I mouth at him real slow "Den-tist. To. The. Den-tist." Then Eli goes all ghostly white and angry. "Geraldine, nothing good gonna come from that doctor. Here, let me walk you on to my house." Straightaway he grabs my arm without permission, holds me tight and we start off some other direction. I try to protest but it's gibberish, and then my jaw really stings. From a passing car it must look like Eli's the Good Samaritan helping a shriveled old broad down the street, but I start sweating under my blouse when I realize I've been half-kidnapped by a Christian Scientist and Lord what will he do with me when I untie this scarf and he sees my jaws open wide like a snake's? He's like to smash me with a shovel, burn me up, and dump the ashes in that creek behind his house.

I go along, pretend I'm a touch more feeble than I am. Meanwhile Eli chats away. "That Doc Parry is a menace and a quack. You know he botched my cousin Darren's root canal? There's something of the devil in him. Somebody oughta turn the doc's own tools on him." That gets me sweating more. With all the talk Eli loosens his grip, so when a truck swings by I do the natural thing and dash out in front of it. I twist and swish my way across the street, my back bent and head low like I'm in a football huddle. Truth is the jaw's got real heavy, weighs me down. I clear the truck—I can move pretty swift when threatened by a Christian Scientist—but the driver screeches to a halt and starts to yell at Eli. I hear shouting but I don't look back, just hoof it over to that dentist at the best pace I can manage, my mouth jostled and aching with every bounce.

✠

I make it around the corner of Lincoln, few blocks down Madison and on to Harding Street. Bent over and wheezing but I'm making it. I waddle past the high school Levi went to before the drugs got into him. I think about all the times I took him in, cleaned his scraped little knees and held him after his momma (I won't own up to her as a daughter) beat his face to pulp. Then what's the boy do but grow up with a trigger-happy temper he liked to turn on me when the chemicals was on him. He had a mean left cuff, but I've been known to take a punch or two in my time. I'd slap that boy back to the Stone Age when he pressed me.

I'm wondering if it's all those brawls with Levi that have yanked my jaw out when I come to Doc Parry's. It's an old split-level house cut around the middle of a cul-de-sac. Not a usual kind of place, but then he isn't a usual kind of dentist, which I'm hoping on as I pound his door and pray to Jesus Doc Parry's seen some similar strangeness before and can tell me all there may be to do.

It's early on a Saturday but not so early he wouldn't be up, so long as he's decent folk. Turns out he is decent since the door opens. He's got a mug in his hand. On the side the mug says "Biloxi Bitch" in big red letters and I think, *Lord, what did I do to deserve all this?* The Doc raises his mug as a greeting, takes a long sip. "Geraldine. I love a good surprise." Coffee drips from the bottom of his mustache, stains it brown, but it's his eye I have a devil of a time not looking at. His left is lazy, an occasional wandering orb that if I didn't know better was always trying to catch a glimpse of something it shouldn't.

Talking isn't an option so I wave, make a few urgent grunts, tug at the end of my scarf and boy if that don't make my jaw feel on fire. I bend over and cradle it. Doc Parry sips more coffee, narrows his one good eye at me. "Good surprise. Come in, Geraldine. Take a load off." I'm so grateful I don't flinch, move quick through the doorway. The jaw is feeling heavier and heavier, like the whole damn world's pulling down on my face, like my head could pop off and roll on the floor. I take slow steps to the nearest chair, collapse myself into it.

Doc Parry turns around slow, takes another sip, which is really two sips since he drinks some on the first toss and drinks more when he sucks in his mustache. It's plain gross and I'm feeling queasy so I try not to think about it but God help me it's such a peculiar little thing I can't look away when he does it. I wonder if this is what it feels like to have a lazy eye, compelled to witness strange matters. I wonder if this is how Levi feels with a needle dug bone-deep in his arm.

"Alright, let's see what you got."

The room feels cold like there's a draught. Doc's waiting room is dim with musty furniture that's ripped up in a few places, little wisps of cotton coming out. Suddenly I'm scared to show him.

"Come on, Geraldine. I've seen it all before."

I get over myself, huff on through to that great dentist's chair, big and puffy like what my brother slept in back when he twitched his neck out and wore a halo for three months. I lay myself down, the back of my head landing with a smack. The office is a calming place. Doc Perry's piping some Beach Boys song real low through an old radio on the counter.

Doc reaches for the knot on the scarf, but I'm not about to let myself be messed with more than necessary. I swat him away and undo it myself, let the jaw down slow. It's like that Jacob Marley scene from every *A Christmas Carol* movie, my bottom lip dropping lower and lower, only there's no creepy music or sound. It's just there. And sore.

When I'm done the jaw reaches to my feet. My cheeks are stretched like old clothes with little waves running through them. Lord, I think, just don't let me end up too ugly. A little ugly's alright, but not too much. Maybe I need a new moisturizer.

Doc Parry sets the mug down on the counter. I was scared he might jump up and stomp me, but he just sits there, pulls on a few of his mustache hairs. "Huh." He bends down to the lower jaw, squints at it and pokes at my rotten tooth. "Weird."

I turn away so I don't see his gawking at me like I've got three heads. My eyes go out the little window in the office. It's a nice day but I get depressed seeing Doc Parry's put bars over the windows, thin little bits of metal, probably meant to keep those manic kids like Levi from busting in and stealing the laughing gas. How must Levi be feeling when every window he sees is like this one, all cut up into little shards so that he never quite gets a complete look at the world. It must grip his heart every time he sees the light, and I get to thinking of where I might've been better with him and his mother, all the things I've done wrong.

When I look back the doc is wagging my jaw up and down, testing out the skin. He clears his throat and stands up straight. He looks so tall in his white coat. I wonder if he ever takes it off. The doc pulls open a drawer and hands me a notepad and pen. It's a simple move but I'll be damned if he isn't sharp.

"When did it start?"

This morning, I scribble out.

"You've no idea what might have caused this?"

I don't pen a reply, just narrow my eyes.

Doc Parry rubs a thumb over his nose, sits down. He puts his hand over mine, and I know it must be bad, tell myself to hang on.

"I believe I got this somewhat figured out—not completely. I can't say what's caused this to happen, but I do know what you got here." Doc Parry's grip tightens on my hand. I get to sweating and I could just slap him to get on with it.

"Geraldine, you're a sin eater."

I give him a good look before writing *A What?*, add a dark underline before I turn the notepad around.

"A sin eater. One who is called to carry the burden of evil and strife for the rest of us. That's why your jaw dropped. I've seen it before."

How do I get rid of it?

"You can't. If you're born a sin eater you'll die a sin eater. You're meant to carry the community's sins."

But what's with this megamouth?

"I imagine you're being prepared to swallow something real heinous. Must be a whopper of a sin." Doc Perry shivers. "My advice: sniff it out and gulp it. See if the jaw reels in then."

I expect this kind of nonsense from a Christian Scientist, but Doc Parry's a relatively reasonable man. I'm agitated and about plain done with him. *What is it I'm supposed to consume with this wobbly thing?*

Doc shrugs, his lazy eye looking out the window. "Beats me. Wait, I got an idea." He runs out the office and returns with a couple of magazines. He holds them up to show off the covers, all with women in various states of undress. "Dirties." Doc Parry goes red. "Don't really know why I keep these around."

Before I know what's what, Doc rolls up the magazines and feeds them into my mouth, shoves them right down like funneling them through a paper shredder. The Doc's so quick I don't have time to protest. I get a stinging sensation in my face, feel the weight of the magazines on my tongue, the strange texture of the glossy paper like that sour taste from licking stamps. The next moment they slide down the back of my gullet and disappear. When I get a bearing on my faculties I leap up, and wouldn't you know that jaw feels the slightest bit lighter, enough that I can carry my back straight. I'm amazed by this lightness, and I have to admit to myself the doc may be on to something.

Doc Parry looks disappointed. "Those sure weren't it. But you can't give up, Geraldine. There's gotta be something pretty damn evil around for your whole face to come unhinged that way. It's your job to root it out and eat it."

I know he might be right but I can't help roll my pupils around. I scratch out on the pad *But how will I know what it is I'm to sin-eat?*

"I haven't the foggiest, but I imagine there'll be signs. Just keep yourself open and ready to understand the signs when they come."

It's hard to call him nuts on account of the eye. It makes a person feel like Doc has some sort of greater line of vision instead of a crappier one. I can't say I'm buying all that the doc's saying, but I also won't deny that the magazines made some kind of difference. I go pale when I think about those filthy little things inside me, wonder where exactly they slithered off to.

I've got a lot to consider for a Saturday morning, so I saddle up my jaw with the scarf. Doc Perry walks me to the door. "Don't go telling the whole neighborhood about this. Whatever you're looking for sure doesn't want to be found. We'll keep this sin eater stuff between us." He winks at me with his good eye and for a second there he looks full-on certifiable. I pat his arm and thank him in my best mumble before I take off, leaving with an easier stride than when I came in, though my mind is anything but.

✠

Before heading home I run by the Dollar General on the corner. I don't say hello or look anyone in the eye, march straight to the back where I grab a pack of pens and four yellow legal pads, the same kind my daddy kept around the house but never used. Doc Perry had at least that one good idea. I'm still not sold on the rest. What's a dentist really know about sin? The man probably hasn't had so much as a tootsie pop in twenty years. Not a drinker. Odd, but clean-cut. Maybe he has a quieter vice, gambling or some such rot. Then I recall the smut rags and a little tremor shakes my whole body, my heels making tiny scrapes on the floor. I'm not sure if it's from the memory of the visit or the magazines.

Tammy Bollinger is up working one of the counters, smiles and gives me a little wave. I'd like to avoid people, but here she's already waved so I can't go to some other register now. Tammy drops her grin when I come closer, but I'm working hard not to notice, quietly setting down my pads and pens.

"Miss Geraldine, are you doing okay? Your mouth there looks a little off. What you got it wrapped up for?"

I'm not known as a liar, but without a second's hesitation my fingers rip into those pens and grab a pad off the pile. *Slipped on kitchen tiles and straight smacked my chin against the washing machine.*

Tammy puts a hand up to her chest. "Don't that beat all." She starts scanning pads. I return the pad I wrote on and feel proud of myself, fibbing on the fly. The register makes its beeps. When she hands me the ticket Tammy leans in real close. I always knew her as a blonde, but now I spy what's natural at the roots, the tiniest bit of brown at her scalp. "Miss Geraldine." Her hands cross over mine. "I know you didn't slip. I'm just so sorry this happened to you." I'm keeping my face blank like I don't know nothing, but inside I'm growing desperate, hoping Tammy knows what I don't, something about this damn jaw and how to get rid of it.

She pats my hand again. "You shouldn't have to take that terrible treatment, not when you've done so much for that boy. Levi should be ashamed. If you need anything at all, just know Fred and I are there for you." Tammy gives my hand a squeeze and lets go. For the first time all day I'm grateful to not be in a talking state, just smile and nod and make my way out of there as fast as I can move.

Not even halfway home and a trickle of sweat runs down my spine. The jaw starts to hurt again like someone's kneading it into tight knots. But it's my mind that's got me churning, all this craziness from Doc Parry, sin eaters and evil and signs. It's too much. Who am I to carry this burden? I'm no spring darling. Who am I to seek out evil and ingest sins? Even if I buy into all this mumbo, I've no idea what clues to look out for. Anything could be a sign. A person could go mad reading signs into every breeze or whistle or petunia or stray cat. A crabapple lies out on the sidewalk, wrinkled, green, moldy on one side. Stopping to look down on the brainy thing, I think, *Is this a sign is this a sign tell me if it's a sign.* The crabapple's squishy when I pick it up and toss it, hit a little bench and feel kind of bad, move along at a faster clip.

It's not fair but I'm angry at Tammy talking about Levi that way. He hit me, sure, but not as a regular thing, and not out of meanness. It was only with the pills in him that he really laid hands on me. He had a rough childhood, that mother of his carting him around while she got her fixes and leaving Levi with god-knows-who when he was just a toddler. Deep down, he's a good boy.

Back at home, I drop the sack on the kitchen counter and am not sure why I fussed with the pens and pads. No one's around but me. Levi's gone now, his mother long since disappeared. Robert passed eight years ago. Funny how little I consider him anymore. We didn't love each other at the end, think we both knew. It was why he spent the last decade of his life in the basement, flopped out in that great green Lay-Z-Boy, not bothered and not bothering much with anything but the TV. Still, I could use a companion about now, even a poor one like Robert. I never did have much of anybody to lean on, only myself. Maybe that's why I was chosen for this, the sin-eating. Maybe heaven needs a lone wolf to do its dirty work.

The midafternoon sun reaches into my front room, but I'm already exhausted from the day, my mouth bunched and wrapped up, shoulders burning. It's all I can manage, to put one foot in front of the other, clopping up the steps like some tired old mule. My clothes'll wrinkle, but I'm so wiped I don't care, just lay myself out on the bed, don't even think about what I'm doing as I untie the scarf. My jaw flies out like a tape measure unspooling across the room. I'm nearly wall-to-wall, mounds of flesh and my big trap open to the world. Lord, I worry for my neighbors. I'm about to snore like thunder.

✠

Seven days I manage to not leave the house, just shuffle around in my bathrobe thinking, praying, and searching for signs. The weird feelings in my jaw come and go, numb then tingling then pain. It's aching so much I consider donning my little sunglasses, scooting over to the liquor store late at night and buying some more dirty mags. When the doc fed me those smuts it gave me a little relief from the pressure, from all this tension coiled up under my skin, but I know that idea's a nonstarter. Probably the damn jaw would open wider, respond to my cheating. Most of the time I keep it tied up and gathered, but occasionally moving about the house I let it go, just drag the silly thing, my chin hitting the floor behind me like some demented wedding train. You'd think it might gather crumbs or splinters from the hardwood, but I haven't noticed any such yet.

Most of my time has been drinking coffee and agonizing about how Levi's getting along. No word from him. I'd like to see him but wonder if it's too soon. He won't leave my thoughts lately. All I do is pace and worry. I went a little off the deep into cabin fever, started watching my neighbors and all the kids passing up and down the streets. Eli's out one morning planting marigolds around his driveway. He spots me through the window and puts up a friendly wave. Panicked, I duck and race up the stairs, take them three at a time. I'm in no mood to explain myself. I hear him knocking and giving out my name, but I don't dare answer. When I finally go down he's wedged a Christian Scientist pamphlet in my front door.

The jaw makes normal chores impossible. Baths take an extra half hour what with all there is to scrub. Dressing is still a hassle. Flossing went clean out the window, though I won't be telling Doc Parry.

The eighth day holed up, a Sunday, I can't stand it any longer. Word of my jaw and Levi must surely be spreading around town, so if I don't go down to Robert's old Baptist church they'll send someone after me, those tenacious little prayer-jockeys. Besides, I need to breathe clean air. Maybe the jaw needs it too, like walking a tiny poodle around the block. I take my time donning a sensible blue dress, match it to a robin's egg scarf. It's a hassle to pull the jaw up but I get it in the end, tie the scarf and mosey off to church.

As soon as those oak doors open, I'm bombarded with sympathy. If I hadn't brought a legal pad I'd have been really loss. As it is I hunch over, wave and manage some kind of smile, though by the congregants' faces I know my grin's not quite right. Holding up the Dollar General excuse works wonders. *Slipped on kitchen tiles and straight smacked my chin against the washing machine. Slipped on kitchen tiles and straight smacked my chin against the washing machine.* The ladies in Sunday School cluck over me with their powdered faces and big moans. But most congregants glance with sad eyes and turn away, leave me alone. I wonder how many are sitting in those burgundy pews thinking like Tammy Bollinger, assuming the worst of Levi.

It's a beautiful chapel, serene with wood pillars, stained-glass windows, and a cute tub area behind the pulpit for baptisms. Smells clean and old. Calmness knocks me back every time I walk in. Love the place, but they're not my favorite folks, these Baptists; they can go judgy on a person quick, without warning. Still I'm tickled to be out of the house.

As I walk down the aisle, Cecil Jacobs reaches out and grabs my shoulder. It's an odd move that'd seem threatening on the street, but here it's supposed to be nice, a set of fingers coming down on your shoulder showing someone cares enough to stop you.

"Geraldine." He smiles and his eyes are hard to discern with those transition lenses he's got. He leans in close to where I can smell his cologne—real top-shelf stuff—notice a few stray hairs peeking out his nostrils. "I was a beater for years. That's why Claire left me, took the kids to Georgia. I know the signs." A trickle slows its way down his cheeks, both sides of his face quaking. The organ plays and people shuffle along to their seats. "Much too late for my family, but I make my amends by helping those like I harmed." Cecil's big hands take a tighter grip on my shoulder. He's about to make a bruise out of me. "Let me help, Geraldine. Let's get you away from that Levi."

If I could speak, I'd let out a torrent on Cecil even my mouth isn't big enough to hold. Here he is putting his own dirt on Levi's back. I know my face is wrinkled and angry, but I'm not in a mood to care. I rip the first page of that pad with a sound that runs through the congregation like a whip crack. Crumpling up the paper, I leave it in Cecil's hands, hope he takes me at my written word, and move on to a quiet seat in the back. The jaw is aching again when I plop myself down.

The music man starts in with hymns, so it's all this standing and sitting, standing and sitting in ways that don't make sense. Of course when we're up we're meant to sing. It's a touch aggravating. Back years ago I came because Robert wanted to. All his friends went here, and he liked being seen. They all think I haven't been in a few years on account of Levi, which isn't true. I just can't stand a one of them.

We sit for good and hear the preaching. Most Baptist ministers are worn and pudgy round the middle. But this one—relatively new—is young and fit. He's one for the theatrics, moving around the stage wearing bright red suspenders with gold clips that flare in the light whenever he raises an arm. I should be taking it in, but I'm too miffed. Instead I pick up my pad and go to town, scrawl out a rant that's as dirty as I dare on a Sunday morning during a Baptist sermon.

Cecil Jacobs is a rotten load of tripe who chased his own kids off with the bottle, a withered pony looking to score with whoever will take his sugar. I've half a mind to saddle him for a ride just to crunch his carrot. The rest of these puffed-up hussies can go suck a musk sack. Should be ashamed, thinking like they do about Levi. The boy ain't perfect, I'll be the first to call it. But I'll be cold dead before I let these here speak against him.

Writing it down is asking for trouble, creating evidence. I could just think the things, but it's so much more satisfying to spill on the page. Besides, I get bored sitting in that hard pew. The mind wanders.

Levi was six when he first came to me from his momma. He had bright red hair then, shiny with a slight curl. He loved this robot-dinosaur toy that he knew how to change into a little man. That dinosaur came with us everywhere, courtrooms and DFS and the ice cream shop. Levi used to gulp down a whole cone before I could pull out my coin purse. Strawberry was his flavor, which I figured was on account of his red curls. As he got older his hair faded to some muddy brown, and though he's still a young man he's already half silver. But to me he's that ice cream boy, licking down a strawberry cone like it's the last one on Earth.

I wish he'd give me a call.

The preacher gets going and you can see he's good, yelling and waving his arms, the congregation focused and giving out the occasional "Amen." He's pacing back and forth, going at it so hard spit sails from his mouth. "Jesus died and was raised in three days. Samuel answered the third call. The Trinity—Father, Son, and Holy Spirit—the mystery of three in one." He's a good speaker, sure, but I can't see all the fuss about him. "Three is a sacred number to Almighty God. He calls His children, sends His signs, in threes."

My back tenses. Threes. It's a message about the message, how I should be looking in on threes, and here I am thinking on nothing but Levi. Then it strikes me: Neighbor Eli, Tammy Bollinger, Cecil Jacobs. Three people now warned me about Levi. I think about the boy nonstop and I can't quite recall but maybe my jaw gets hurting every time I think about him too. It rushes in on me like cold water. I took in magazines, but could I be asked to sin-eat a person?

No. Not Levi. I'll open my wide maw and swallow anything but Levi.

This whole crazy week starts making too much dark sense. I leap and shuffle out the church door while the preacher's still going. Those church hens give me looks, but they were giving them before. I need to get home, consider things but it's hard when this flappy jaw hurts so much, bends my back, me hunched over down the street, the weight of the whole town and all their sins on me and I could keep walking, bite my tongue and feel the blood move through my teeth and bare it all for them if only for Levi, if it didn't have to be my one boy, who—mean as he can be—is the one good thing in my world.

The mouth is throbbing by the time I reach my street. I've never been more grateful Eli is a Christian Scientist and they have their own Sunday services, couldn't stand to see him or any other human soul at the moment. The door jams a bit but I force my way in and collapse in a rickety chair. I don't even have to undo the scarf as my jaw falls out the back of it when I sit down, unrolls its floppy way to the floor.

An old cordless rests in its holster on the kitchen counter. I know it's a new age, but I never could get rid of my home number. When I was a girl the telephone was everything, my line to friends and the world outside my home. Hard to imagine severing that, even if now all I get are pollsters and salesmen. They don't normally leave messages, but I see that blinking red light and it feels like some evil snake watching me. Not two hours ago it would've filled me with joy instead of the drowning I get when I hit the button and hear Levi's soft voice.

"Hey, Nanna How you doing? I miss you and I'm sorry it took me so long. I've done alright so far considering. Thinking on my sins. I just got you on my visitor's list and tomorrow—I was hoping—tomorrow is visiting day for my block. I know it's an hour or so from the house, but if you want you can come by around nine. It sure would lift my spirits to see you. Hope you come, Nanna. Love you."

I'm a sin eater. How can a boy be a sin? How can a whole person who eats ice cream and reads comic books and loves tinkering with his drum set even when it drives his grandma crazy, how can that whole being turn into sin? I don't know if I can do it.

My jaw makes a high pinching sound, like turning a screw into a tight block of wood. It's a sharper pain than I've been used to, some new and intense wave that leaves me gasping. I peek down and there's my mouth gaping open with that rotten tooth at the bottom, the thing gray and sticking out more than normal. My gums tighten hard like concrete until the tooth shoots up, makes a noise like popping a cork, then lands on the kitchen floor, a little stream of blood behind it. Taking deep breaths from the pain, I'm terrified for what this all means. Could I not eat the sin I'm called to, just live with this hanging thing the rest of my days? Or is the tooth a sign of worse to come, that the God of those Baptist will keep torturing my worn body until I follow through and swallow the punching, loving junkie that I raised as my son?

As the pain subsides in waves my fingers let go of the counter I didn't know I'd been gripping. The sun's still peeking in strong, just early afternoon, but I'm worn. Weighed down by the task. I never was vain, so I don't mind the jaw taking my looks. Gabby as I can be, the no-talking hasn't bothered me like I thought it might. But give up my son, have him disappear like those magazines, send him to some invisible hell inside me. I make my way to the stairs and stumble up them, my chin slapping against every step.

I've been known as a complainer, but I tend to do the right thing. I didn't love my husband, but I kept my vows, a wife good and faithful. I raised Levi as my own when that daughter of mine wouldn't. I tolerate them around town that annoys me to no end. So I reach the bed, lay myself out on it sideways, don't try to roll the jaw up or straighten out, just start off toward sleep, but before I get there I pray to God.

"Okay. You win. I'll do it. But afterward I will hate you forever."

✠

A long night filled with bizarre dreams: Doc Parry in red suspenders, singing at the top of his lungs and both eyes revolving like planets; dirty-mag women dancing in a circle around Eli, the Christian Scientist; Robert, grown to the size of a mountain, thrown back and snoring away in his Lay-Z-Boy. Light's beginning to show at the edge of the sky when I start awake to a pounding headache three cups of coffee tossed down my gullet don't shake. I don't eat; if I'm hungry it might be easier. I pick a nice floral dress and a red scarf, tie it neat, jump in my Oldsmobile and take off with the sunrise. The morning starts with pleasant weather, but as my tires crunch their way to the prison clouds roll in. Everything turns gray, and I'm grateful to God for that. At least He won't be mocking me with clear skies and sunshine. A dark day should look the part.

The drive's easy but long, leaves me too much time to mull it over. The jaw feels tight and sore, my stomach rumbling as the great concrete castle comes into view. Seems like miles of barbed wire circling the whole building twenty times. At least Levi won't have to be here anymore, in this evil place.

The visitors' lot is completely empty. Must not be too many get-togethers on a Monday morning. As I walk up I worry those guards will confiscate my pad and pen, maybe make me take off the scarf and then Lord knows what'd happen. But they buy my excuse, the new one I wrote down—*Tripped and fell cheek-first on a rake while gardening*. I almost wish they'd screen me more, make me turn and go home. The sin-eating never leaves my mind. Walking down that dim hallway, it occurs to me I'm about to do exactly what all these prison guards fear, help Levi out of here, though I'm not sure he's going anywhere better.

The visitors' center is a big room with five long rows of tables, each table with a strip of yellow tape down the middle. I'm the only one here and I'm escorted in by a guard. He's got a hefty paunch going, looks a bit dead round the eyes. "Bunch of lonely guys here today," he tells me. "Your boy's lucky." That really starts me burning, and the jaw throbs. But I keep myself composed, give the guard a nod before he steps out to the hallway, starts playing on his phone. I pick a spot in the middle of the visitors' center, park myself in a chair, and wait. It's all this sitting and waiting that sets an agony into my gums.

Levi comes in on the far side, a guard right behind him. The boy's head is down, facing those cuffs around his hands. He's skinny, or at least he looks it in that orange suit. His hair's grown out a bit since I saw him last at the courthouse, but as he lifts his head to face me I see a few streaks of red still hidden in there. His skin's splotchy and pink. When he gets up to me neither of us says much, just looks at the other all pitiful as the guard shoves Levi into the chair on the other side of my table, explains a few rules, and walks out. I thought these guards was to stay and keep an eye out, but they don't seem to give a flip. I'm desperate for one of them to step back in, keep me from doing this.

Levi reaches a hand right to the line and I see a mesh of purple sores all up his forearm, the mutilated spots on his face. It's easier focusing on these things, on the ways he looks like sin. He makes a whimpering sound, lets out a big sigh. "Nanna, what have they done to you?"

I'm a bit taken back that he asks about me first, but I settle myself and look angry, jab with my pen at the pad, *Tripped and fell cheek-first on a rake while gardening.*

He reads it slow, runs his hands over his whole face. "Oh, Nanna. I don't deserve none of this."

I'm seizing on that, the boy's selfishness, his lack of repentance. He's pathetic, all scabs and pity, a moldy soul. I'm ready, Lord, I'm ready. I'll never forgive myself, but I'm ready. Dart my eyes, make sure no guards are looking. I'm working the handkerchief knot with my fingers. I suppose I've been preparing for this most my life. More than anything, I'm hungry.

The inmates aren't allowed to touch across the line, but Levi pulls my hand away from the scarf, cups it in his two, and kisses it. Kisses my old, wrinkly hand. "I don't deserve a Nanna like you looking out for me, really I don't. I hate myself for what I'm putting you through." Levi wipes his nose on his sleeve, reaches up and actually strokes the side of my cheek, through the handkerchief, kisses my hand again. "Tripping while gardening. That's my fault too. I should be out doing your gardening. I'm the one should be taking care of you."

Levi's never been a saint, rarely grateful. Yet here he is, treating me with an affection I didn't know was in him. There's tightness in my jaw, the skin pulsing, wanting to get the job done. But I don't move, refuse to move.

"I'm learning a lot about myself in here. It's good for me. I've hurt so many people. I'm a sinner, a real low-down sinner. And you," he faces me again and I feel weak, "you're an angel for keeping me alive."

I speak it inside, to myself and to God. *No. I will not eat for you this sin.*

Every tense muscle in my body softens. I start scratching on that pad fast as my digits can move. I tell him about the lemongrass beef and dill buttered carrots and pumpkin pie I got planned for when he gets home. I lay out the future I see for him, going to college, driving a pretty red car, working at the hospital across town, earning a good wage and a happy life. I shower that boy with every word of comfort I know, that his best days and self are still there, within reach, at the horizon. Levi reads it upside-down soon as I write it and sobs until his thin chest is shaking. He starts in on these big wails that cause the guards to poke their heads in and out.

Levi stops me and grabs my writing hand, reaches across the table and pulls me into a hug. Those guards see but don't mind. "I love you, Nanna. I'll stay strong and be there for you when I get out. Then we'll tackle all that gardening together."

✠

In all my years with that boy, I couldn't have imagined a better visit to prison. God, the jaw, the signs, and the whole damn town had prepared me to eat him, cast him into a void. But hard as I tried I couldn't do it. Though the visit was wonderful, a sadness washes over me as I drive home, unfulfilled and still with this thing, this huge, floppy jaw dangling from my face. And desperately hungry. Speeding down the highway through the beginning sprinkles of a solid storm, I think about how no one is ever going to see my face again, really see it. Before I wouldn't have much cared but you just don't know until it happens, how you'll feel when your jaw goes flimsy.

Now I'm a failure to my holy purpose, a no-good sin eater. Maybe the jaw will stay with me forever, maybe it'll cause me excruciating pain as I decay and die. Pulling up the drive, I'm almost laughing at it all, how I went, failed, and ended up hating God anyway.

Stepping out of the car as the rain falls hard, I sense the house looming, the idea that I can't go on like this around town and will have to become a hermit, that once I walk through that front door I'll rarely come out again. The very thought makes me lean on the car, the jaw surging with heat and weight again. This jaw will be my life, a burden I'll carry for Levi's sins until my final resting day.

"Geraldine!" The rain's smacking hard against the hood of the car, a metallic echo carrying out from it, but I hear my name called over the noise, turn and see Eli, drenched in his own driveway, waving his big hands and walking over to me. I'd rather see Satan himself hoofing toward me, so I turn to make a dash for the house, but my whole face surges with such a breathtaking sting I stop, brace myself again on the car and wait for Eli.

He reaches me and through the water dripping down his face I can see him look frustrated. "Geraldine, why are you out in the elements, and still with that mouth problem? I told you not to go to that dentist." Eli grabs my arm again, pinches it between his huge fingers and starts leading me away, toward his own home. "Here, we'll get you all dried out then take you to someone who can really fix you up, a Christian Scientist. Since you don't have Levi around, I'll look out for you. Not that the boy ever did you any good."

Eli starts dragging me and though I don't want to go I'm resigned to it, the idea that he might bring me before all those other Christian Scientists, maybe chop me up into little bits.

After a few steps some spasm carries through me, and toes-to-temple my whole body goes numb and tingling with a kind power. I hear a high-pitched squeal, the flow of my own blood and the crunch of my own bones as I grind Eli to a halt. On its own my mouth hisses, and I feel a strange wind moving through me. I reach out and take hold of Eli's forearm, his grip no match for mine. He looks at me puzzled but I'm already lifting him, my arm crackling and stretching to some mad length. Heat pulses beneath my skin, turning the rain to steam. Eli's clear off the ground, brown loafers dangling and starting to kick with the realization that something is happening here, that neither of us is in any form of control.

167

I hold Eli up with one hand, dangle him like a treat. With the other hand I untie the scarf and let loose my great and terrible sin-eating jaw. He panics and struggles against my arm but it's no use. He's already being lowered into it, my mouth vibrating and giving out this deep bellow. The jaw spills wider than its ever been, responds to Eli, moves around him as I finally let go, hear the rush of him scream and fall, and like a cresting wave of water the lips surround him and fall away, a giant heap of flesh and gums left hanging over wet leaves with not a man in sight.

Gathering up my jaw like a fallen dress, I bunch it in my arms, make a dash for my front door. I'm moving faster than I have in years, like I'm a happy kid again in a race on the playground. Slamming the door behind me, I let down the flaps of jaw, so many wrinkled layers they almost take up the whole living room. The couch is comfy when I lie back to think on it, but I can't stay still for long, all this energy coursing through every part of my body, I'm seizured with inexplicable joy. The jaw hasn't shrunk—seems bigger than ever—and I'm still not sure it'll ever go down. But for the first in a long time I feel alive and so light I'm floating on a cloud in the darkness of my own home.

ACKNOWLEDGMENTS

To everyone at University of Alaska Press and University Press of Colorado. Special thanks to Krista West for all her hard work on the cover and layout design. And thank you to Ian Dooley for his beautiful cover photo.

To Julie Iromuanya, for believing in this book. I hope to live up to your own brilliant words.

To my school teachers, who were always deeply supportive of my writing: Ms. Sasche, Ms. Davis, and Ms. Warren. Special thanks to Ms. Didomenico, who cryptically told a 16-year-old me "if your future does not involve writing, the world will suffer." A strange thing to tell a student, but Ms. D motivated me more than she knows. I hope it's not too grandiose to imagine this book might alleviate some small portion of the world's suffering. Thanks, Ms. D.

To Susan Swartwout, Steve Barthelme, and Andrew Milward, for teaching me how to write and how to teach. You're the ones who showed me how to turn writing from a hobby to a discipline. You showed me grace and caring by seeing me for my potential rather than my skills at the moment. Thank you.

To the Split/Lip team for their infectious passion and enthusiasm, especially Kristine Langley Mahler, my partner-in-crime for five years and counting.

A special shoutout to my MSA students, my kids who aren't kids anymore: Andrea, Dawson, Sydney, John, Erykah, Lexi, Katt, Isabel, Jaycee, Bethany, Xavier, Bradley, Shelly, Jordyn, Leo, DeeDee, Michael, Chris, Amory, Marley, Trinity, Delaney, and Nick. Brilliant writers, and even more brilliant human beings. With hard work and grit, you are each destined for greatness. (Angry water helps too.)

To my Southern Miseries squad, Susan, Mike, and Joe. Your support and friendship means more than I can say. Brothers and sisters forever.

To Bill and Lynne Lofton, for showing us deep kindness when we needed it most. We are eternally grateful.

To the magazines that took a chance on the work in this collection: *Carve, The Knicknackery, Puerto del Sol, The Cimarron Review, CutBank, Sycamore Review, Midwestern Gothic, Permafrost,* and *Pacifica Literary Review.* Special thanks to David Gates and Adam Johnson for plucking my work from contest piles.

To my literary inspirations: Louise Erdrich, Kevin Wilson, Marlon James, Kelly Link, Sequoia Nagamatsu, Roxane Gay, and Charles Yu. Your wisdom and insight is priceless beyond measure, and I'm deeply fortunate that I get to witness and learn from you.

To a large host of supportive colleagues and friends in Washington, Mississippi, Missouri, and beyond. Specifically Joshua Smith and Alyssa Bennett Smith, Ryan Harper and Lynn Casteel Harper, Kent Quaney, Fae Dremock, Jamie Paige, Robbie Hargett, Davida Marion, Anna Purol Powell, Heike and Laurence Philipson (and David and Emma!), and the Glasgow gang: William, Jordi, Daniel, Beata, and Tony. You may not even know the ways in which you've helped this book come alive, but I could not have done this without you.

To Glasgow, that city like a warm drunken hug.

To my family: Mom, Dad, Whitney, Matt, Sydney, Jess, Tyler, Henry, Owen, and Charlotte. Thank you for always supporting me, even if I've had weird dreams that have taken me to far-flung places.

Finally, to Richie. This book is a love letter to you. Salamat sa pag-mamahal mo sa akin.

CALEB TANKERSLEY is the author of the chapbook *Jesus Works the Night Shift*. His writing can be found in *Carve, The Cimarron Review, Hobart, Sycamore Review*, and more. He is the managing director for Split/Lip Press and lives near Seattle. *Sin Eaters* is his debut collection.